THE MUDFLATS
OF
THE DEAD

Also by Gladys Mitchell

SPEEDY DEATH
MYSTERY OF A BUTCHER'S SHOP
THE LONGER BODIES
THE SALTMARSH MURDERS
DEATH AT THE OPERA
THE DEVIL AT SAXON WALL
DEAD MAN'S MORRIS
COME AWAY DEATH
ST. PETER'S FINGER
PRINTER'S ERROR
BRAZEN TONGUE
HANGMAN'S CURFEW
WHEN LAST I DIED
LAURELS ARE POISON
THE WORSTED VIPER
SUNSET OVER SOHO
MY FATHER SLEEPS
THE RISING OF THE MOON
HERE COMES A CHOPPER
DEATH AND THE MAIDEN
THE DANCING DRUIDS
TOM BROWN'S BODY
GROANING SPINNEY
THE DEVIL'S ELBOW
THE ECHOING STRANGERS
MERLIN'S FURLONG
FAINTLEY SPEAKING
WATSON'S CHOICE
TWELVE HORSES AND THE HANGMAN'S NOOSE
THE TWENTY-THIRD MAN
SPOTTED HEMLOCK
THE MAN WHO GREW TOMATOES
SAY IT WITH FLOWERS
THE NODDING CANARIES
MY BONES WILL KEEP
ADDERS ON THE HEATH
DEATH OF A DELFT BLUE
PAGEANT OF MURDER
THE CROAKING RAVEN
SKELETON ISLAND
THREE QUICK AND FIVE DEAD
DANCE TO YOUR DADDY
GORY DEW
LAMENT FOR LETO
A HEARSE ON MAY DAY
THE MURDER OF BUSY LIZZIE
A JAVELIN FOR JONAH
WINKING AT THE BRIM
CONVENT ON STYX
LATE, LATE IN THE EVENING
NOONDAY AND NIGHT
FAULT IN THE STRUCTURE
WRAITHS AND CHANGELINGS
MINGLED WITH VENOM
NEST OF VIPERS

Gladys Mitchell

THE MUDFLATS OF THE DEAD

LONDON
MICHAEL JOSEPH

First published in Great Britain by Michael Joseph Ltd
52 Bedford Square, London WC1
1979

© 1979 by Gladys Mitchell

All rights Reserved. No part of this publication
may be reproduced, stored in a retrieval system,
or transmitted in any form or by any means, electronic,
mechanical, photocopying, recording or otherwise,
without the prior permission of the Copyright owner.

ISBN 0 7181 1818 9

Typeset by Saildean Ltd. Printed and bound by
Billing & Sons, Guildford.

Contents

PART ONE

Colin Palgrave

1	The Coast Road	9
2	The Mudflats, Saltacres Strand	16
3	Ménage à Quatre	25
4	Interlopers	37
5	The Dead	48
6	Serious Doubts	59

PART TWO

Dame Beatrice

7	Discreet Enquiries	71
8	Two Interviews	81
9	Further Information	90
10	The Witness	99
11	The Old Mole	109
12	Palgrave Again	118
13	Interim	130
14	The Flat-Mates	139
15	The Mudflats, London River	147
16	Faint but Pursuing	161
17	A Dead Man Speaks	170
18	The Mudflats, Ampletide Sands	181

To
Gwen Robyns
with love and admiration

'And to be read herself she need not fear; Each test and every light her Muse will bear, Though Epictetus with his lamp were there.'

John Dryden

PART ONE

Colin Palgrave

CHAPTER 1

THE COAST ROAD

'The irresponsive silence of the land,
The irresponsive sounding of the sea.'
Christina Georgina Rossetti

Palgrave was in search of inspiration; that is how he put it to himself, although not to those of his circle who had asked him how he intended to spend his holidays. What he meant was that he needed a plot for his second novel. He had been overjoyed when his first book had been accepted, the more so when he signed a contract which called for another two novels. The signing, however, was six months old and, strive as he might, not a single idea which could form the basis of a second novel had come into his head.

'And if not a second, how on earth can I manage a third?' he had asked himself miserably on the eve of the school's seven-week summer vacation, as he stared at the rows of empty desks in a form-room he had grown to hate. He had been reminded of himself at the age of nine, seated in a similar room, but in a pupil's desk, not at the teacher's table. The end of term examinations had been over, sports day had come and gone, the little boys were restless and fidgety, the form-master was bored and had run out of subjects for the weekly essay. Falling back on a well-tried but never very successful formula, he had told his class to choose their own subjects for composition. Having stifled the groans and the reproachful cries of 'Oh, *sir!*' which this shifting of his responsibilities had evoked, Palgrave's form-master had spent the next twenty minutes on the boys' reports and in trying to find alternatives to *Works well on the whole* or *Could do better* or the even less helpful, from the child's or the parents' point of view, *Finds this subject difficult.* Failing in this object, he had laid the blotter over the reports and resorted to his usual practice of strolling up and down between the rows of desks to see how his embryo and mostly unwilling authors were getting on.

When he had reached Palgrave's desk he had found an unhappy small boy staring at an almost blank page. Palgrave had written the date in a fair, round hand and had added: *My Own Choice of Subject.* Otherwise the page was empty.

'Well, Colin, old lad,' the master had said, 'what *is* your own choice of subject?'

'Please, sir, I can't think of one.'

Here he was again, once more in the same boat.

That time, however, rescue had been at hand.

'What about *Myself on Sports Day?*'

'Please, sir, I wasn't there. It was my father's holiday and I was taking my fortnight.'

'And had the good sense to miss the maths paper, I remember. Well, *imagine* you were there. You can do that, can't you? Pretend you won the four hundred metres.'

'Yes, sir. Thank you, sir.'

'All part of the service, so get a move on. The lesson's half over.'

But now there was no kindly assistance forthcoming and Palgrave's dilemma had reached the stage of giving him sleepless nights and a daily sensation of near panic.

'I *can't* have dried up already!' he told himself despairingly. 'If I have, bang goes my dream of giving up this miserable job and becoming a professional writer.'

He jettisoned his gloomy thoughts after giving a last glance of loathing at the ink-stained empty desks, smiled at the cleaner as she came in with her tea-leaves, broom and pail, and went whistling down the stone stairs to the masters' lobby. Cheerful masculine voices were exchanging jests and holiday farewells and from the adjoining lobby came the inexorable clacking of female voices from the distaff portion of the staff.

Palgrave took his mackintosh from its peg, responded to one or two friendly quips and then went into the staffroom to collect his briefcase and a couple of books he did not want the cleaners to handle, and found the room in the occupation of his particular buddy, a young man named Winblow, who was clearing out a locker. He desisted when Palgrave came in.

'Oh, hullo, Colin,' he said. 'Thought you'd gone. You're off on the sacred quest tomorrow, then, are you?'

'I suppose so.'

'Meet me at the Dog and Duck at six and I'll buy you a drink and wish you luck.

Meet me at gloaming at the Dog and Duck,
And in their witches' brew I'll wish you luck!
How's that for a rhyming couplet?'

'Lousy. All right, I'll meet you when I've done my packing. Thank God for the invention of the internal combustion engine! One doesn't any longer need to travel light.'

'No. Even room for a dead body in a four-seater's boot. Why don't you write a thriller if you're stuck for a plot?'

'Because a thriller has to *have* a plot. That's the one thing it can't do without. See you at seven, not six. I'll have all my gear marshalled by then, I trust. Six is too early to get all my packing done.'

'Don't forget the kitchen sink!'

Winblow was in his confidence, but in reply to other staffroom enquiries about his holiday plans, Palgrave had said that he was going to take his car and tour the roads, stopping for the night at any place which pleased him and staying longer if the neighbourhood was especially attractive. What he did not say (but it was his real objective) was that he wanted to find a setting which would suggest a theme for his second book.

He had thought of Cornwall and Wales, but it seemed to him that what he required was a part of the country which he did not know at all, so that he came to it with a fresh mind and no preconceived ideas. He thought, too, that it ought to be lonely, desolate and mysterious, although he wondered whether there could be such a locality on an overpopulated island.

However, by the beginning of his second week he began to think that he was on the track of what he wanted. His progress had been leisurely and he had been held up in Colchester for a couple of days while the car was in dry dock for repairs to a faulty clutch. In any case, he had decided that up to about a hundred and twenty miles a day, following by-roads and avoiding the motorways, would take him as far as he wanted to go in the four weeks he had allowed himself for research, and on the Monday of the second of these weeks he was on a coast road which left a large and a smaller town behind and ran almost due west, linking a number of small villages whose names he knew only from the motoring atlas which he kept in the car.

Again according to the map, they were seaside villages, but once he had left the cliffs behind him, the road was often two miles or more from the sea. The high cliffs had been formed of sand and gravel, deposits of the Ice Age, a series of moraines brought by the action of glaciers, but, after the first few miles, these cliffs had given place to huge banks of pebbles as the sea had receded from the land and left its own desposits behind. Between these pebble-ridges and the sand-dunes blown together by the bitter winter winds were the vast sea-marshes which accounted for the coast road having been made so far inland.

Palgrave pulled up just outside a village landmarked by a windmill and a magnificent church. He left the car and walked over the marshes. A channel broad enough to be called a creek ran seawards and the marsh itself terminated in dunes sparsely covered with marram grass. Beyond these was a brackish lake, its shores sun-dried, but a trackway at one end of it led down to a flat, muddy-looking shore.

On the dunes he found sea-holly and the green-white flowers and waxen leaves of sea-sandwort, and behind him the marshes themselves were covered with the pink and grey of sea-lavender and the small, yellow flowers of sea-purslane. He returned to the car and had a look at the map. A few miles further along the road there should be a larger village. He began to think he could do with some beer and bread and cheese.

The road made a long arc, almost a semi-circle. It crossed a small river to which the narrow creek he had seen formed the estuary. To his left were slopes too inconspicuous to be called hills. To his right were the seemingly never-ending marshes, sad and uninviting to some eyes, but to Palgrave's they represented exactly what he thought he was looking for. Their melancholy charm, their appearance of being divorced from civilisation, of being part of a lost world, enchanted him. Surely they would suggest a plot for his book, he thought.

'A combination of Thomas Hardy and Mary Webb,' he decided. 'What I shall aim at is a mixture of romantic tragedy and country lore, and, of course, I shall include the mystery of "the unplumbed, salt, estranging sea." To hell with the moderns. I shall write a classic. All I need is a basic idea.' He began to feel more cheerful than he had felt for months, and, as he gazed ahead and nothing was in his sights but the road following the bases of the green slopes and, to his right and ahead of him, nothing but the never-ending prospect of the marshes, he began to sing.

Then he saw another church tower in the distance and realised that he was approaching a village he had marked as his stopping place for a ploughman's lunch. He slowed down as he approached it. He had not thought of making it his headquarters while he searched for what he thought of as inspiration, but there was always the possibility that it might prove to be the very setting he was looking for. He drove even more slowly, looking also for a pub.

The village, which was called, reasonably enough, Saltacres, consisted of a long, straggling high street with narrower streets opening off it. At one time it had been a place of some importance, a sea-port for boats to and from the Netherlands, but its harbour had gradually silted up until the channel which had once formed an estuary of some size was no longer suitable for anything but small yachts and motor-cruisers and the village had become a backwater, although, as evidence of more prosperous days, it retained a seventeenth-century town hall, now used once a week as a covered market, and the vast and lofty church he had already seen on his approach.

The houses and cottages were of all periods, a heterogeneous collection which had contrived, owing to the passage of time and the vagaries of the weather, to make of itself a picturesque, acceptable whole. The main street had not only retained its cobbled pavement, but many of the dwellings were of banded flint patterned after the fashion of a countryside which boasted no other indigenous stone.

'This will do me,' thought Palgrave, pulling up in front of an inn. 'Get a drink and a snack here and ask where it's possible to stay. I must see more of this place.'

The landlord was unhelpful. There was no hotel in the village; he himself had no accommodation for staying guests; he doubted whether there was a cottage to let on a fortnightly basis. Palgrave finished his meal and decided to stretch his legs again before he continued his journey. He was deeply disappointed. He felt there was nothing he wanted more than to stay in this off-beat village.

He walked along a roadside cobbled with unknapped pebbles of flint, turned towards the sea and came out once more on to the apparently limitless marshes. To his right, on the only spot of rising ground apart from the low hills behind the village, was the fifteenth-century church with a tall, square tower and a lesser, but still impressive, beacon light on the seaward end of the roof. Before him, but a long way off, was the pebble-ridge thrown up by aeons of relentless tides and between it and the spot where he stood stretched the grey-green landscape of unutterable desolation, interspersed with streams and ditches.

'If only I could find lodgings here!' he thought sadly.

To his left, a kind of causeway led to a little wooden bridge which crossed a narrow part of what seemed to be the main channel of a small creek which widened rapidly as it approached the sea. Palgrave followed the slightly raised path and stood on the bridge.

Palgrave's work was in a London suburb, but he had spent many holidays in the Highlands. In that part of the country it was the mountains, 'still and blanched and cold and lone', which dominated the landscape and dwarfed and threw out of perspective all other natural features, but here, despite the apparently endless stretches of the sea-marshes, the dunes, the pebble-ridge and even the sea itself, it was Fitzgerald's 'inverted bowl we call the sky' which dominated everything.

The endlessness of the flats, sad marshes, the ever-winding, ever-widening creek, the water-colour brushwork of the creaming, retreating tide, were all subservient, insignificant, unimportant and almost, it seemed, unnecessary in the face of that vast, unfathomable, bland, uncaring vault overhead. The quality of the light, too, was amazing. Palgrave was reminded of a holiday he had spent in Greece. How he wished he were a painter, not a writer!

The little bridge was made of broad planks covered with a fine layer of windblown sand. There were stout uprights on either side, joined together by an equally sturdy wooden rail. Palgrave leaned on this to survey the scene. Below him the creek, narrow here, was running out fast. At a confluence between the main stream and a lesser channel, a sailing dinghy was stranded on a mudbank, the bare mast of the boat lying slantwise, cutting across the umber banks of the creek so that the blue and white burgee at the masthead was almost lost against the blue and white of the wispily clouded sky.

Palgrave was about to leave the bridge and continue his walk towards the dunes when he was aware of a girl who was approaching the bridge. Having no mind for company while he was mentally roughing out a description of the scene for his book, he walked on, quickening his pace, but from behind him she called out, 'Hi!' and began to run.

Palgrave slackened his pace, then stopped and waited for her to catch up with him. She was a thinnish, leggy creature unattractively dressed in a large, long, shapeless sweater of the type which used to be called a Sloppy Joe. Faded blue jeans came halfway down the calves of her bare brown legs, and a pair of muddy, canvas-topped shoes brought her over the bridge to Palgrave's side.

'Hi!' she said again, panting a little as she joined him. This second exclamation was not a call to him to stop, as the first had been. It was a greeting, American style.

'Hi!' he replied, in the same idiom. With her tousled, unkempt, uncared-for elf-locks, her suntanned face and limbs, her coltish gracefulness, she could have been an elemental, a spirit of the place, a creature born of the marshes, the dunes and the sea. Her eyes were bright and avid, her lips as curved, as pure and as sensuous as those of the Citharist Apollo in the Naples museum. Except for her eyes, which were giving him the summing-up a woman gives a man she is meeting for the first time, she could have been a hermaphrodite. Palgrave's first reaction to her was one of dismay and dislike. He wanted neither her conversation nor her company. There was no civilised way of making this clear, however, so they strolled together alongside the creek and soon left the little bridge behind them. The girl began to explain her reason for accosting him.

CHAPTER 2

THE MUDFLATS, SALTACRES STRAND

'Forlorn the sea's forsaken bride
Awaits the end that shall betide.'
John Davidson

'Didn't we see you in the pub just now?'

'Probably. I was there.' Palgrave had been aware of a fresh young voice coming from one of the alcoves, for the inn was furnished with settles which had facing seats like miniature railway compartments. He himself had taken one of the high stools at the bar, and the voice had been his only clue that he and the barmaid and the landlord had not been the only occupants of the place. 'I had a ploughman's lunch before I decided to push on.'

'Where to? Where are you going?'

'I don't really know.'

'We thought we heard you asking about finding somewhere to stay.'

'Yes, I did speak to the landlord when he came to relieve the barmaid. I rather fancied this village for a stop-over, but there doesn't seem any chance of it. He doesn't let rooms.'

'How would you like to muck in with us? The others sent me chasing after you to find out. We've got a cottage here. We could put you up, if you like.'

'But you don't know anything about me.'

'What does that matter? We're all human.'

'According to some of the things I read in the papers, I'm not too sure about that, apart from the fact that I'm a keeper in a blackboard zoo.'

'A schoolmaster? I should never have thought it.'

'I hope that's a compliment. I'm also what they call a rising young novelist.'

'Published?'

'Certainly. As a matter of fact, I'm collecting material for my next book. That's why I thought this place might give me what I'm looking for, a setting.'

'Well, you've had my offer. Take it or leave it, only make your mind up so that I can let the others know. We'll have to get in some more bacon and eggs and things if you're coming to stay.'

Palgrave glanced sideways at the girl. Not more than sixteen or seventeen, he thought. He was not enamoured of the conclusion that he was being invited to share a holiday cottage with pop-enthusiastic and probably guitar-playing and certainly record-playing teenagers. To have them in school was bad enough. He certainly did not want to spend part of his vacation with them.

'What others?' he asked.

'Only Adrian and Miranda. Adrian designs wallpapers and paints flowers and things on cups and plates. Miranda teaches part-time at the art school and paints seascapes. They're married and quite old – in their thirties, I think. I'm sure you'd have a lot in common with them.'

'Thanks. I'm twenty-six.'

'And a bachelor?'

'For what it's worth, yes.'

'Wouldn't she have you? You look a sort of one-man-one-woman type to me.'

'As a matter of fact, *I* broke the engagement.'

'Did she play fast and loose? You should have given her a beating and told her to behave herself.'

'I broke the engagement because I wanted to write, that's all.'

'Under your own name?'

'Certainly. I've a very appropriate name for a writer.'

'Yes? Tell me, and then I can introduce you properly to Adrian and Miranda when you meet them and I can also ask for your books at the library.'

'I'm Colin Palgrave.'

'Camilla Hoveton St John.'

'That's a village, not a surname.'

'I know. It sounds nice, though, doesn't it? When my

parents died I adopted it. You don't get far in the art world calling yourself Thomasina Smith.'

'You're an artist, then, like your friends?'

'Art student only, but I persevere. Well, are you coming back with me to meet the others?'

'I – well, look – I don't want to commit myself to anything.' He stood still and looked about and around him. Behind was the village, mellowed by distance to a not unpicturesque jumble of brown, grey, white and dirty red; above him a limitless expanse of sky; all round him the grey-green level of the sea-marshes; before him the marram-topped mounds and undulations of the sand-dunes, and beyond them the pebble-ridge, the muddy-looking beach and the gently moving green, blue, silver of the glittering, sun-warmed sea. He turned to the girl and, as their eyes met, she laughed.

'All right, Mr Cautious,' she said. 'You haven't committed yourself to anything – yet. Come on. You never know your luck.'

He took to the married couple at once, especially to Miranda. She was plump, comely and kind, a blonde who would be prettier, he thought, if she could contrive to lose a little weight. As though to redress the balance, Adrian was very tall and noticeably thin. He was a quiet man, soft-voiced and courteous, but although he and his wife welcomed Palgrave, no mention was made of a bed for him at the cottage. It was clear that the girl had been lying when she had told him that the others had sent her chasing after him.

Just as he was thinking of taking his leave and driving to the next town to get a room for the night, an opening came and Camilla took immediate advantage of it. Miranda asked where Palgrave was staying and he replied that he did not know.

'He would like to stay in this village,' said Camilla.

'But at the pub they held out no hope,' said Palgrave, 'so I had better be pushing on.'

'Can't he stay here? There's the studio couch,' said Camilla.

'Stay here? Well, yes, if he doesn't mind our rough and ready ways and people having to pass through this room to reach the front door,' said Adrian, looking at Miranda. She nodded.

'It will be good for you to have another man for company,' she said.

'Good for me, too,' said Camilla pertly. 'Besides, he will pay a quarter of the rent and help with the chores.'

'Oh, hang it all!' said Palgrave. 'I can't impose myself on people I've only just met.' He was embarrassed by the way this extrovert girl had taken charge of the situation and committed the married couple to a course which probably they had no wish to follow. Miranda reassured him.

'We shall be delighted to put you up. Can you pay ten pounds a week? That would be for bed, breakfast and supper. We have a snack at the pub if we bother about lunch at all, so that would be extra.'

'Well, it's awfully good of you. Could I stay for a fortnight?'

'Not quite a fortnight,' said Adrian. 'My lease of this cottage is up on Saturday week, but you could stay until then, if that would suit you.'

'So ten pounds for a full week, and one pound fifty a day for the rest of the time,' said Miranda in businesslike tones.

'Profiteering!' said Adrian, laughing.

'It's awfully good of you,' said Palgrave. He took out his wallet and produced the notes. 'I'll go to my car and get my things, then.'

'I'll come with you,' said Camilla.

'What are we to call you?' asked Miranda.

'My name is Colin Palgrave.'

'Colin, then, and our name is Kirby, but to you, please, we are Adrian and Miranda.'

'And I am Camilla,' said Camilla, taking his hand and leading him towards the door. 'Where will you park your car? There's a wide bit of the road a little further on. You would find it handy unless you want to leave it where it is.'

'I'll get the bed made up while you are gone,' said Miranda.

'You know,' said Palgrave, when he and Camilla were outside the cottage, 'you had no right to wish me on to those people.'

'Oh, nonsense! Miranda will be glad of your money. They only asked me to join them because they wanted some help with the rent. They don't really like me all that much. Do *you* like me, Colin?'

'I don't know yet, do I?'

'When we've dumped your suitcase or kitbag or whatever, will you bathe with me? Usually I have to bathe alone because the other two can't swim.'

'Now, look here, young woman, the reason I'm staying here is that I want a setting for my book. I'm not just a casual holidaymaker. I shall be very busy, I hope, most of the time. I shall be taking notes and getting the feel of this place. I don't want interruptions and I don't want company on my excursions. Sorry to be so blunt, but it's better to get things straight.'

'All right, but don't you forget that if it weren't for me you wouldn't be staying here at all.'

'True.'

'So will you swim with me just this once, by way of saying thank you?'

'You're a persistent little so-and-so, aren't you? This time, however, you lose out and that for the best of reasons. I don't have my swim-trunks with me. They're in the car and I'm dashed if I'm going to rout them out now.'

'Keep your underpants on. If we sprawl out on the dunes afterwards they'll soon dry off.'

'I don't have a towel, and I hate being sun-dried.'

'Dry yourself on your shirt, then. Any more stupid objections?'

'Yes. I'm too full of pork pie and beer to go swimming. Here's my car. Get in and show me this parking space you mentioned.'

'There's no hurry. Wouldn't you like to buy me a drink? The pub will keep open for another half hour and Miranda won't want us back until she's found you some bedding and put the room to rights.'

The last thing Palgrave wanted was to involve himself further with the girl, but he followed her into the pub and twenty minutes later they returned to the cottage with his suitcase. The studio couch had been opened out to make a double bed and he had a suspicion that Miranda and Adrian had stripped the sheets from their own bed to put on his. There were no pillows, but plenty of cushions, and in reply to an enquiry he said that he was sure he would be comfortable. He added that he would like to change his clothes.

Accepting the hint, the other three went out, Camilla to bathe, Adrian to search the marshes and the shore for plants and small sea-creatures which would suggest wallpaper patterns, Miranda to make pencil sketches of the church. He watched them go past the window and then he unpacked his belongings, put on flannel trousers, an open-necked shirt and a blazer, thrust a notebook into one of the pockets, hid his wallet and cheque book in his bed, and walked out on to the marshes.

He had reckoned without Camilla. She was waiting for him and she fell in beside him as soon as he appeared. He said nothing and affected not to notice she was there. The afternoon was hot. Very soon he took off his blazer and slung it over his shoulder. They tramped over coarse grass and sea-lavender until they came to the sand-dunes. Here they ploughed their way through the deep, soft sand and the marram grass and when they reached the top Palgrave sat down and took out notebook and ballpoint. Camilla lay down beside him, propped her chin on her fists and gazed out towards the pebble-ridge and the sea. Palgrave frowned at the blank page of his notebook.

'I'm being very good, don't you think?' said the girl.

'You'd be a lot better from my point of view if you were somewhere else.'

'Tell me all about yourself. I'm a student of human nature and I've never met a rude man before.'

'I'm not rude. I'm here to write and I don't want company, that's all, especially the company of adolescents. I get quite enough of that at school.'

'Are you a good schoolmaster?'

'Competent, I suppose.'

'Shall I tell you about myself?'

'No thanks.' He got up, returned his notebook and ballpoint to his pocket, picked up his blazer and scuffled his way downhill towards the beach. He thought at first that the girl was not going to follow him, but he was clambering and sliding over the smooth pebbles when she caught up with him. When he had cleared the ridge he found that there was a shallow lake left by the last tide. The girl came cascading down the pebble-ridge and sat down on the sad-looking shore. It seemed to consist of more mud than sand, and exhibited numberless casts and depressions made by lugworms, for although the tide had turned it was a long way from the high-water mark.

Camilla took off her shoes. She stood up, walked on the squelchy shore and called back to Palgrave:

'At least take your shoes and socks off! Don't you love to feel the mud between your toes?'

'Not particularly. Where I usually spend my holidays the walking is over heather and the peat-bogs. Oh, well, if you want to, let's swim.'

There was nobody else about. They stripped off, the girl revealing that she was wearing a bikini under the loose sweater and the calf-length jeans, and were soon splashing their way through shallow, sun-warmed water.

The girl was a competent swimmer, but Palgrave soon outdistanced her. The bottom shelved suddenly and he found himself in deep water, although the waves were small. When, having had enough, he swam back and waded ashore, the girl was still disporting herself. He climbed back to the sand-dunes and lay spreadeagled to dry off. After another quarter of an hour she joined him. He saw her coming out of the water and before she reached him he had pulled off his still damp underpants and was into his flannel trousers.

Camilla apparently had no such inhibitions. Unconcernedly she took off her two bits of almost non-existent nonsense and lay down. From the colouring of her skin Palgrave deduced that sunbathing was among her ways of passing the time in these desolate surroundings. He took a pipe and matches from the blazer which was lying beside him and sat clasping his knees and smoking as he gazed out to sea.

Beforetime he had spent a holiday at a resort on the Solway and had seen the unexpected speed with which the tide there came in and receded. Here it did not come up so fast but, even so, he was interested to watch as, more swiftly than he would have supposed, half the mudflats were covered.

At the cliff-top town which he had left that morning, the incoming tide took a slightly slanting direction from north-west to south-east, but here, less than forty miles along the coast, this trend seemed to be reversed. He put this down partly to the direction of the wind. Although it was warm, it blew fairly strongly, caressing his bare shoulders and ruffling the girl's dark hair.

He looked across at her. Her face was turned away from him with her head resting on her rolled-up sweater. Her back was childishly thin, the shoulder-blades slightly prominent, the waist scarcely narrower than the hips. The back was enticingly hollowed like that of a young gymnast and her legs were long and straight. She looked defenceless, elemental and, in spite of the immature body and the careless boyishness of the whole pose, seductive and desirable.

Palgrave shook his head at his own thoughts, knocked out his pipe on his tin of tobacco, rolled loose sand over the dottle, stood up and put on his shirt and blazer. He rolled his underpants into a ball and stuffed them in his blazer pocket, disposed of his pipe, tin and matches in the other pockets and said,

'I'll leave you to put your things on. I'm going back now.'

'Oh, wait for me,' she said, 'and I'll make you a cup of tea.'

Palgrave turned his back while she dressed. She caught his hand when she was ready and held on to it, swinging his arm a little as they walked, more slowly this time, across the marshes and along the banks of the creek. They crossed the plank bridge, took to the causeway and made their way towards the village.

They did not converse. The girl hummed something monotonous and, to his ears, tuneless, but he sensed that she was happy. He himself was filled with a languorous contentment after his bathe. It came from the enchanted confluence of the sun's warmth and the sea, and he felt at peace with all men and even in some kind of comradeship with the determined girl. He was still certain that the invitation to stay at the cottage came from her and from nobody else, but in his state of euphoria he felt sufficiently grateful to her not to make any attempt to put an end to the hand-holding, embarrassing though he found it.

'After all, she's only a kid,' he thought, 'and she's probably lonely.' On impulse, when they were drinking the tea she had made, he said, 'Do you really think I'm rude?'

'No, it's my fault. I shouldn't make a nuisance of myself, but the other two are so sufficient unto themselves that it really isn't much fun for me down here. I'm glad you've come. Adrian and Miranda have been married for years and years, but they're still in love with one another. Are you married, Colin?'

'You know I'm not.'

'Engaged?'

'No. I told you! I was engaged at one time, but an author is no sort of a husband, so I broke it off and now she has married somebody else.'

'Was she nice?'

'Very nice.'

'Do you have regrets?'

'Sometimes; not very often.'

'Do you ever see her nowadays?'

'No, thank goodness, although they live in the same London suburb as I do.'

'The other two won't be back for ages. I'll just wash up these tea things and then we can go to bed for a bit.'

'Not on your life! How old are you?'

'Nineteen. Nearly twenty.'

'I don't believe it.'

'It's true. Are you prudish?'

'I'm a schoolmaster.'

'And I'm an art student.'

'You're a sinful little beazel. Any more of your nonsense and I leave on the dot and go on to the town. I mean it. You damn well behave yourself, or else you'll make it impossible for me to stay here.'

CHAPTER 3

MENAGE A QUATRE

> 'One for sadness,
> Two for gladness,
> Three a wedding,
> Four a death.'
> *Anonymous*

The cottage comprised the sitting-room, now allotted to Palgrave, a kitchen and a small scullery downstairs, and two bedrooms at the top of a steep staircase. From his front window Palgrave could look out over the marshes. He moved a small table into the window and borrowed a chair of the right height from the kitchen and set out his notebook, a sketch-pad and his portable typewriter and continued to wait for the inspiration which still did not come.

At first there was little to disturb him. The Kirbys were as good as their word and, except for passing through his room to go out or to come in, both of which they did quietly and expeditiously, they did not speak to him unless he spoke first. For the first two days Camilla followed their example, although he guessed that she directed pleading glances at the back of his unresponsive head as he sat at his table in the window making notes and a sketch plan of the immediate neighbourhood.

By the third day, however, this good behaviour on her part broke down. She came downstairs before dawn and, while he was still asleep, she wriggled her way on to the studio couch beside him. He woke to find a naked nymph who clung to him with such determination that he had to use what seemed to him brutal force to break her stranglehold and deposit her on the floor, where she knelt sobbing with her head buried in the table-cover which was doing duty as a quilt and, so far as he could make out, threatening to blackmail him for seducing his girl pupils. She was clearly beside herself with frustration and disappointment.

Palgrave got up, put on trousers and a sweater over his pyjamas and went out into the chilly half light which preceded the sunrise. When he had walked off his irritation and had rehearsed in his mind what he would have to say to Camilla when they next met, he returned to the cottage with a half resolve to leave it immediately after breakfast and look for lodgings in the town which he knew was only a few miles away.

'And a damn nuisance *that* is!' he said severely to the girl, walking with her to the little bridge in the middle of the morning.

'Oh, Colin, don't go!' she said, leaning on the sturdy handrail and gazing not at him but across the expanse of the marshes. 'I didn't mean any harm. It was only a joke. You needn't be so stuffy. I don't wonder you chose to be a schoolmaster! You're just an old stuffed shirt. Are you going to tell Miranda and Adrian about me? I shan't do it again, you know. I don't like puritans and you're not very attractive, anyway.'

Palgrave put a hand on her thin, childish shoulder and pulled her round to face him.

'Look,' he said, 'I don't want Miranda and Adrian mixed up in this, and I don't want to go. What I *do* want is to settle to my book and get this place and my main characters down on paper, that's all.'

'Am I one of your main characters, Colin?'

Palgrave laughed.

'Not if you don't behave yourself,' he said. 'I'd like to put you in the book, but as an older, more sensible girl, I hope. I don't mind swimming and walking and talking with you – in fact, all those things will help me to round out the character I want to build up – but beddery, and all that, is definitely *out*. You wouldn't be a bad kid if you gave yourself half a chance, but giving me the rush of a lifetime is not going to do either of us any good. When I bed a woman she's got to be just that – a woman – not a half-baked art student hardly out of her teens. You're still wet behind the ears, my child. You save your antics until you've grown up a bit. Then perhaps one day somebody will fancy you enough to do the pursuing instead of you having to do it all. That will be the day!'

He was trying deliberately to make her angry. He did not succeed. She took his hand and said,

'Yes, teacher. I'm sorry. I won't be naughty again.'

As the end of the week approached he felt the beginnings of his old despair. The conditions were right, the weather was right, the doleful scenery was right. Another *Wuthering Heights* ought to be under contemplation, but no Muse approached him to murmur in his ear those vital sentences which would get him off the mark and start him on the *opus*. He had already settled upon Adrian, Miranda and Camilla as three possible main characters, but how to use them in a story, how to manipulate them, was more than he could determine.

What was worse, it soon became clear that, however sincere the welcome he had received from the married couple, they had had an ulterior motive for taking him into the cottage.

Finding himself alone with Miranda one afternoon when she had asked permission to paint in his room and the other two had gone on to the marshes, Camilla to make some impressionistic daubings, Adrian to roam the foreshore in search of more of those specimens, either of flora or fauna, which apparently he needed for his work, Palgrave pushed his notebook aside and said:

'How do you come to team up with Camilla? If I may say so, she doesn't seem quite your cup of tea.'

Instead of answering his question, Miranda said, in what seemed an inconsequent way:

'My Adrian is a good man.'

'Yes? Why shouldn't he be?'

'He *is*, I tell you. But that girl!'

'I know. I've had some.'

'Are *you* a good man, Colin?'

'I hope so. Why?'

'Camilla needs a husband.'

'Very likely. Most girls do.'

'She has a private income, not large, but permanent, you know. She would not be a financial burden on a man.'

'That's as may be, but, so far as I'm concerned, I've enough on my plate already without taking on a young nymphomaniac.'

'She would not be like that – not if she had a man of her own.'

'Well, frankly, Miranda, I'm not in the market.'

'Do you have a girlfriend?'

'Once. Not any more. She married.'

'Oh, I am sorry! I shouldn't have asked.'

'She thought I was too self-centred. It was while I was writing my first novel. I needed all my faculties.'

'Well, of course, I understand your point of view. Art is a mistress. No wife can hope to compete with her. Of course you had to put your novel first.'

'Yes, but the girl didn't think so. Sometimes I wonder if that's why I can't get down to any more writing. There's a blockage, and I think she is the cause of it. You see, it was I who broke the engagement.'

'It would be nice if you had taken the same fancy to Camilla as she has taken to you.'

'Well, I haven't.'

Miranda sighed and squeezed out a dollop of green paint just as Adrian, bearing a jam-jar containing low forms of aquatic life, returned to the cottage.

'Why are you painting in here?' he asked.

'Because Colin is lending me part of his front window. There is the view I want from here, but it's too windy to sit outside today. I am not breaking our contract. I was not intending to interrupt his work. I did not say a word for more than an hour, and then he spoke first. Now I come to think of it, he asked me a question which I did not answer.'

'It doesn't matter now,' said Palgrave. 'It was an idle, impertinent question, anyway. Where did you leave Camilla?'

'Oh, your question was about her, was it?' said Adrian. 'I carried some of her things for her and saw her settled down to her sketching, but I don't think she did very much work. The last I saw of her she was talking to one of the summer visitors.'

'A man, of course,' commented Miranda.

'Well, she would not trouble herself to talk to a woman, still less to stroll towards the village shops with one.'

'I hope she won't be a nuisance to the poor man.'

'So long as she is not a nuisance to me, I'm afraid I don't mind in the least who else she afflicts.'

'Colin wanted to know why we had brought her with us. The fact is, Colin, that we often take one or more of the art school students away with us in the summer. We quite like young company and, as I teach part-time, I'm able to give them some hints about their work. Camilla begged us to let her join us this year, and at the time we saw no reason to refuse. I'm afraid, though, that we grasped at the idea of having you join us. It really was most unfair considering that you had come here to work on your novel. How is it coming along?'

'It isn't, so far. Inspiration is absolutely lacking.'

'It will come,' said Miranda comfortingly. 'When it does, you won't be able to get the words down fast enough.'

'I don't think that's my style of writing. I weigh up and discard and alter. I'm very painstaking.'

'So am I,' said Adrian, 'but when Miranda finds a subject she likes, she slaps it on to the canvas like a man slapping creosote on to a garden fence.'

'You should never be skimping with oils,' said Miranda, making a quick dab at her huband's nose with a brush full of green paint. Adrian picked up her paint rag and wiped his face. Lifting up the jam-jar, he said:

'I have had some success today, I think, but I wish I had some transport. Further along the coast there are freshwater marshes. The specimens would be different there.'

'I must take you in my car,' said Palgrave, without committing himself to a definite promise.

'Would you? I'll show you the kind of things I do.' He took himself and his jam-jar upstairs and returned with a portfolio. From it he took some water-colour sketches and some pencil drawings. He named the subjects as he displayed them. 'Yellow flag, water violet, marsh pea, marsh woundwort, marsh sow thistle, and this is one which not everybody knows, the rayed nodding bur-marigold. Of course not all of them came from these marshes.'

'They are exquisite,' said Palgrave sincerely. 'Really lovely work.' So indeed they were. Botanically correct in every finely finished detail, they were also delicate, beautiful, sensitive works of art.

'Thank you,' said Adrian simply. 'By the way, if, when you are going down to bathe, you should come across a specimen of the peacock-worm – ' he made a quick sketch on a blank sheet in his portfolio – 'I wish you would let me know. It's a lovely creature, but it feeds underwater. It's a brownish-coloured tube – that's the worm – and these tentacles I've sketched can be pink, red or violet-coloured. So says my book, but I've never seen an actual specimen. I'd like to see what kind of design I could make from it.'

'I'm not terribly good at spotting marine animals except jellyfish and crabs, and those for the best of reasons,' said Palgrave, 'but I'll do my best.'

'Thank you. Oh, and if you should see this – ' he made another rapid sketch – 'I should be most awfully glad. It's called the brittle star. They are five-armed, like an ordinary starfish, but they leave the most fantastic patterns on the sand. The photograph I was shown was taken in Pembrokeshire, so they may not inhabit the beaches here, but you may be luckier in spotting things than I am.'

'I doubt that very much.'

'I want my supper,' said Miranda. 'I think we won't wait for Camilla. The food is salad and things, so she can have hers when she comes in.'

They sat on, after supper, and chatted until Palgrave suggested that his room was both larger and more comfortable than the kitchen. By ten o'clock Camilla still had not come in, so the couple went to bed. Palgrave sat at his window and tried to concentrate on a plot which would involve his three companions. The best he could do was to envisage Adrian falling in love with Camilla, but, even if he used this most unlikely opening, he could not see where it was going to lead him, or how it was going to bear the weight of the thousands of words and the score or so of chapters which would have to follow this less than auspicious beginning.

At a quarter past twelve, while he was still sitting there, but this time with the light on, Miranda came downstairs fully dressed, opened the front door without a word to Palgrave, and went out. Adrian, in his dressing-gown, came down five minutes later.

'I tried to persuade her not to bother about Camilla,' he said, seating himself on the studio couch, 'but she says we are responsible for the girl. I don't see that. Camilla opted to come here with us and she is of age, so why should we bother what she's up to?'

'I don't see how Miranda is going to begin looking for her at this time of night,' said Palgrave.

'There's a song and pop dance thing at the pub tonight. Miranda thinks she has gone to it.'

'It would have been over long ago, surely?'

'That's what I said.'

Miranda came back and sat beside her husband. He looked at her and raised his eyebrows. She shook her head.

'She has never stayed out like this before,' she said. 'I hope she hasn't been out in somebody's car and they've had an accident.'

'If she picked up a lift in somebody's car, she probably got what she's been asking for,' said Palgrave.

'I know. But, Colin, sometimes they kill the girl afterwards.'

'No such luck where Camilla is concerned,' said Adrian, 'so stop worrying. The bad pennies always turn up.'

'Oh, Adrian, I don't think she's a bad penny, not really.'

'A little defaced and debased, perhaps,' said Palgrave. 'And now, if you don't mind, I'd like to go to bed.'

'Oh, Colin! Of course we're sitting on it! Adrian, help him open it out and we'll make it up for him.'

At three in the morning there was a heavy thunderstorm. In the middle of it Camilla came in. She was soaking wet. She put on Palgrave's light and began to take off her dripping garments and drop them on the floor. Her entrance did what the thunder had failed to do. It woke Palgrave. He sat up, blinking in the light.

'Hey!' he said. 'What do you think you're up to? Get the hell out of here, and p.d.q., or I'll give you what I wanted to give you the other night when you managed to climb in on me.'

'Oh, Colin, I'm cold and so tired.'

'Up you go. We'll discuss your sad case with the others in the morning.'

'Just a minute while you get me warm?' She came towards the bed. Palgrave got out of it, walked over to his suitcase and took off the strap which held it together against a broken fastening.

'Ready when you are,' he said, giving the strap an experimental flick through the air, 'and it won't be quite the warming you have in mind.' Camilla gave a coquettish little shriek just as Miranda came down the stairs.

'What happened to you?' she asked fiercely.

'Nothing at all. Somebody gave me a lift into the town, we had dinner and then there was the usual engine trouble on the way back. It might have happened to anybody.'

'Oh, go to bed,' said Miranda. 'Leave those wet clothes in the scullery. I'll see to them in the morning. I'm glad you're all right.'

'*I'm* not. I hope she's caught her death of cold,' said Palgrave. 'If she has, what a blessed relief that will be to one and all!'

He spent the next morning walking over the now spongy marshes. The creek was brimming and was wider than he had seen it before. The water was shadowed with grey which began to turn to silver and then to glints of gold as the sun rose. His wanderings took him as far as the pebble-ridge. It was clear that the holiday season was getting under way, for all the moorings in the creek had been taken up by the smaller yachts and he could see, when he scrambled to the top of the ridge, that several larger craft were anchored offshore, their dinghies either hoisted up on deck or riding behind them.

He came down from the ridge and found a track, muddy and waterlogged after the thunderstorm, which led to the church. Once past the church he decided to take to the road and walk to the village with the windmill which he had passed on his way to Saltacres. Miranda had made a painting of the windmill and he wanted to study the romantically situated little building for himself. As he had become rather too fond of saying since his first book had been published, all was grist which came to a novelist's mill, and he was still hoping that something, somewhere, would bring him what he still thought of as inspiration.

The village, with a mile of marshes between it and the sea, was larger than, when he had passed through it in his car, he had supposed. He explored its ancient streets, found a good road which led down to the beach, looked at the outside of the church but did not go in, and made what inspection he could of the windmill, but discovered that it had been co-opted as part of a modern house. Time passed. He found a small pub near what had been the harbour and jotted down notes and sketches while he had a beer, and then he made his return journey to Saltacres.

He had brought a map with him and learnt from it that there was an alternative to going back by way of the road. It involved a far longer walk than his outward one, for it meant taking a broad causeway which led down to the shore, following another which ran almost parallel with the beach and then taking a long cast across the marshes on another causeway which would bring him out about a quarter of a mile east of Saltacres church.

Just before he reached this last causeway, which turned in a southward direction away from the beach, he saw two people paddling. They were laughing, pushing one another and kicking up the water. One he recognised immediately from the back view. It was Camilla, clad as usual in her jeans and shapeless sweater. The man who was with her was a stranger to Palgrave, but certainly not to the girl for, as Palgrave passed behind them, but twenty yards or so inland, he saw him swing Camilla up, toss her in the air, catch her again, kiss her and then, to an accompaniment of her squeals, dump her into the shallow water. She suddenly hooked the man's legs from under him and had him floundering beside her. They both yelled with laughter.

To his own amazement and self-distrust, Palgrave found himself furious because of these antics. He quickened his pace and turned on to the homeward causeway, but fancied that their laughter pursued him.

When he reached the village he turned into the pub, as usual, for his midday snack and found the place taken over almost entirely by yachtsmen. He looked around for Adrian and Miranda, but they were not present. The bar was noisy and bonhomous, but there was nobody he knew. He managed to edge his way to the bar and put in his order, but ate his bread and cheese and drank his pint as quickly as he could. Then he went back to the cottage and sat down at his work table. He enlarged the notes he had made, typed them out, made a list of possible titles for his book, hoping that one of these titles would set the *opus* in motion, but gave up in despair and decided to go for a swim. The tide was still running out, so he searched the mudflats it was leaving behind and hoped that he might come upon the specimens of marine life which Adrian had sketched for him.

Tiring of this pursuit, he went back to the sand-dunes, took off his shirt and lay out in the sun. The warmth and the lassitude which followed his long walk of the morning soon sent him to sleep. He woke to find Camilla seated beside him, her arms clasped round her knees.

'Hullo,' she said. She sounded deflated and tired. No wonder, he thought. He sat up and gazed out to sea. 'I'm sorry about last night,' she went on. 'Can't we be friends?'

'I don't think you're capable of it,' he replied. 'You can't even keep your promises, can you?' He did not tell her that he had seen her already that day. Again he was conscious of the fact that the emotion her antics had conjured up in him was not disgust but sheer sexual jealousy. 'I'm a dog in a manger,' he told himself angrily. 'I don't want the blasted girl, and yet I'm not willing that anybody else should have her.'

'A penny for them,' she said, putting her hand on his knee.

'You'd be wasting your money,' he said. On the following morning, but with a much later start to his walk, he explored the green countryside of the low hills behind the village. When he got back to the pub he found that, although it was less crowded than it had been at the previous midday, it was still virtually in possession of the yachtsmen. They were crowding the bar, so when he had secured his snack and his drink, he looked around to find somewhere to sit down. He found an alcove which was occupied only by Miranda.

'May I?' he asked, seating himself opposite her.

'Oh, Colin, how nice!' she said.

'May I get you a drink?'

'No, I have had what I wanted. I was just about to leave, but now I will stay and talk to you. It was good of you to lend

Adrian and Camilla your car to go over to Stack Ferry. I did not want them to go together, but Adrian is so anxious to explore those freshwater marshes that I said nothing except that I was grateful to Camilla for taking him – he does not drive and the car was lent to Camilla — '

'But it wasn't!'

'You did not lend it to her?'

'Of course I didn't! I don't allow anybody else to drive my car. Suppose she has a crash and busts it up!'

'That girl!' exclaimed Miranda, for the second time in his hearing, but this time with greater emphasis. 'She declared that you had promised she should borrow it because you were out walking and would not need it yourself today. Oh, Colin, I *am* so sorry! Adrian and I were doubtful, but she swore it was all arranged between you, so for Adrian the temptation to believe her was too strong. There is no transport that he can hire from here, you see.'

'Well, I must hope for the best, I suppose.' Palgrave tried to contain his anger, but could not. He escorted Miranda back to the cottage, put on his swim-trunks, and slung a towel around his shoulders. Still in a state of bitter anger, he took to the causeway, crossed the plank bridge where he had met Camilla for the first time and, walking and running, made his way down to the shore.

The soft warm muddy sand was pleasant to walk upon. Disregarding the dangers of swimming on an outgoing, treacherous tide, he ran into the rapidly shallowing water until he found the sand shelving beneath his feet.

When he got back to the cottage, exhausted and with legs which seemed to be made of jelly, he found that Miranda was still alone. She was seated by his window completing the picture she had begun from the same vantage point on the previous day. She did not look round as he entered, but when he collapsed on the studio couch and gave a great sigh of exhaustion she put down her brush and came over to him.

'What have you been doing?' she asked.

'A damn silly thing, and nearly got myself drowned. The bloody tide carried me out, and when I thought it was time to get back to shore I found there was such a vicious undertow that I began to think I would never make it.'

'You were angry about your car. People do foolish things when they are angry.'

'Well, my first fine frenzy has washed itself away, that's one thing. So long as Camilla hasn't damaged the car I'll forgive her. I shall give her a piece of my mind, of course.'

'You do that. You must also put your feet up and I will make us both a cup of tea.' She was so comforting and the tea was so welcome that he said, when he had drunk it and she had gone back to her painting:

'I say, Miranda.'

'Yes, Colin?'

'No need to tell Adrian my car was taken without my permission. I mean, if he's had a good day, no need to spoil it for him.'

That Adrian had had a good day there was no room for doubt. He was full of enthusiasm and gratitude. He had found a beautiful specimen of the sea-pea – 'not the marsh-pea, Colin, but *lathyrus japonicus,* you know, not *lathyrus palustris.* I have painted one before, but not one so perfect.' Then a fisherman had shown him a lovely marine creature which he had not seen before, the opossum shrimp. 'Not a true shrimp, Colin. This one is not edible. It is only used for bait. It looks like a shrimp and is the most exciting Cambridge blue on top and white underneath. It swims in estuaries and is very active. It is in movement most of the time and does not stay on the bottom, as true shrimps do. I have made sketches and colour notes and now I shall work out my design.'

He was so happy and had enjoyed himself so much that, more than before, it seemed to Palgrave that it would be desecration to say anything about the unlawful use of the car. It did occur to him, however, to wonder what Camilla had been up to while Adrian had been pursuing his own interests.

CHAPTER 4

INTERLOPERS

'Why did my Summer not begin?
Why did my heart not haste?
My old Love came and walk'd therein,
And laid the garden waste.'
Arthur O'Shaughnessy

Camilla accepted Palgrave's scolding meekly, but said at the end of it that 'poor old Adrian' had been 'so pathetically keen' to get to Stack Ferry that she thought, 'Colin, darling', that nobody would mind if she borrowed the car.

'I didn't like to follow you on to the marshes and *ask*,' she added virtuously. 'You don't seem to want me to do that.'

'You didn't want me to refuse to lend the car to you, you mean, you sneaky little devil,' said Palgrave. 'Anyway, I don't know how you got hold of the keys.'

'You're such a sound sleeper, darling. It was quite easy. I nipped into the parlour in the early hours and felt in your pockets.'

'Thanks for the warning. I'll be more careful in future.'

'May I swim with you this morning, just to show you forgive me?'

'I'm not swimming today. I went in on an outgoing tide yesterday and had a job getting back. I am not too keen on going in again so soon.'

'I ought to have warned you. The bathing is safe enough, but not when the tide's going out.'

'So I discovered. Why didn't you mention it?'

'I thought a good swimmer like you knew all about things like that. I suppose you did know, but you were mad with me because of the car and that's why you did it.'

This was so true that Palgrave did not contest it.

'Be seeing you at supper,' he said. 'I shall take the car out myself this morning and put temptation out of your way.'

'We did top up with petrol at Stack Ferry,' she said plaintively, 'so now you can stop being nasty. We didn't hurt your old car!'

Adrian's description of Stack Ferry, apart from his eulogies concerning the marine biology and marsh botany of the place, had made Palgrave think that a day spent in exploring what had once been a famous and important harbour might well be worth while, for at last he was prepared to believe that he was not to get any help with his projected novel from among the mudflats of Saltacres.

If he liked Stack Ferry and there was reasonably priced accommodation to be had there, he decided to make a booking for the following week, when Adrian's lease of the Saltacres cottage in any case would expire.

He thought he would make a full day of his preliminary survey, so he made his own breakfast before the others were up, went along the street to a broad part of it where he had parked his car, and set off. The road still kept its distance from the sea and skirted the low hills, but the scenery gradually altered. There were several bridges to cross and at the foot of the hills there were small lakes. On the seaward side several rough tracks led down to the marshes, but petered out long before they reached the sea, and after he had passed a round barrow on the landward side, he went through a village which had a perfect little Norman church, which he visited. A few miles further on he came in sight of the town.

He drove on past the parish church, an edifice dedicated to St Nicholas, sure sign of the town's former connection with the Netherlands, and then found a signpost which direc'ed him either to turn sharp left for the next village or sharp right to reach the town centre. The road to the right, which he took, soon narrowed. It passed a coastguard station, skirted a considerable creek (still a couple of hundred yards wide, but obviously much silted up since the time the Dutch trading vessels had been able to sail into the town) and then the road swung right again and he could see the church tower once more.

He found a street parking place, locked the car and set out

on foot to explore the town. It was an interesting and picturesque old place, important enough, in spite of its vicissitudes, to have a railway station and a bus station, and in the middle of the town there was a long green open space still known as Archery. Around it were the houses, Georgian and Queen Anne, which once had belonged to wealthy merchants and ship-owners, but were now either decayed or turned into flats.

Narrow streets led down to the quay, and there were so many holiday makers about that Palgrave became doubtful as to whether he would be able to get accommodation for the following week. He found an ancient, pleasant inn for his mid-morning beer and made enquiries.

Did they let bedrooms to holidaymakers?

Yes, they did. What would he require?

A single room for a week or possibly a fortnight.

When would he want to take it up?

From Saturday afternoon, but he was not quite sure of his plans. Would they make a tentative booking?

Yes, if he cared to leave a deposit. The town was beginning to fill up and they could let the room without any trouble.

When he was shown the room Palgrave had his doubts about this. He was conducted to it by way of the public bar and a narrow dark staircase which could lead nowhere but to the quarters usually allotted to the staff. The room, approached by a passage lighted only from overhead, was cramped and low ceilinged and contained a single bed of the least possible width, a chest of drawers, a chair and half a dozen wire coathangers hung on a brass rod behind a curtain. There were no facilities for washing. Palgrave pointed this out.

'No room for a fitted basin,' said his guide. 'Bathroom on the next floor. I'll show you. Anyway, this is the only room that isn't booked up, so it's take it or leave it, I'm afraid, sir.'

Palgrave paid the modest deposit, went down to lunch and found the meal satisfying and well cooked. In the afternoon he cruised around in his car, visited a stately home, had his tea there, dined at The Stadholder, his inn, and got back to the Saltacres cottage at just after nine. Here a surprise awaited him.

The others were out – at the pub, he supposed – but his

studio couch had been opened up and the bed made, and on that bed were a pair of alien pyjamas and a nightdress, and at the foot of the bed two suitcases not his own. He could make nothing of this display, but he found it disquieting and waited impatiently for the return of Adrian and Miranda.

When they came in, Adrian looked apprehensive and Miranda flustered and embarrassed.

'Oh, you're back, Colin,' she said, with an attempt at brightness. 'Would you like some supper?'

'I've dined, thanks. I say, Miranda, what's all this?' he waved his hand at the suitcases. Miranda waved her own hand in agitation.

'I know! I know!' she wailed. 'But, Colin, what could I do?'

Adrian shot an apologetic glance at Palgrave and, in the craven manner of most men faced with a domestic tangle, muttered something about changing into his slippers and went upstairs.

'Well,' said Palgrave, 'what could you do about what?'

'There has been an overlap in the letting. These people say they have it in writing that they booked the cottage for a fortnight from today and *we* have it in writing that it is ours until midday on Saturday. Adrian, always despicable, poor boy, when there is trouble, says we must move out and go home. I said to him — ' Palgrave sat down on the bed and she came and sat beside him and took his unresponsive hand – 'I said what about Colin? What about Camilla? Both pay their way and expect to be here for the rest of the week.'

'True enough. And so?'

'I do not give way. We have as much right to the cottage as these other people. I suggested that there should be a compromise and after a little argument they saw that there was nothing for it but to agree.'

'How many of them are there?'

'Only the two of them, Colin, a doctor and his wife.'

'So what's the compromise?'

'Well, a simple one, really. The woman can sleep in Camilla's room. There are two beds in there. You and the man – he is young and clean and charming – will share the studio couch.'

'I'm damned if we do!'

'Oh, Colin, it is only for a night or two.'

'If it was only for *one* night the answer is still the same.'

'Well, the only other thing,' said Miranda, 'is for the new ones – they are Londoners and very nice people – to have the studio couch, and for you to take the other bed in Camilla's room. You could rig up a blanket as a screen between the beds. Adrian would help you.'

'And how long is that going to keep Camilla out of my hair?'

'Oh, Colin, you said you could deal with her and I'm sure you can.'

'Look, Miranda, I see your difficulty but I want no part in helping you out of it.'

'At least come into the kitchen and be friendly. We will all talk it over with them and see what is best to be done.'

'Oh, they're in the kitchen, are they?'

But when he went into the kitchen a further shock awaited him. He had raised a startled query when he had learnt that the interlopers came from London, but reflected that, after all, London is a large and sprawling place. All the same, he had lived in it for several years and taught at one of its schools. It would be just his rotten luck that these people might even be the parents of one of his pupils. Meeting parents on Open Days or at Parent Teacher Association meetings was bad enough. To encounter them on holiday was intolerable. Something told him that disaster loomed.

He could not refuse to accompany Miranda to the kitchen, but there the situation was even worse than he had anticipated, for he recognised one of the newcomers at once. The girl was Morag Kintyre, to whom he had been engaged and whom he had discarded in favour of his Muse. She greeted him calmly, but with a thrust from a verbal dagger which she did not even know she was holding.

'Hullo, there, Colin!' she said. 'When are we going to see your second book reviewed? We've been looking out for it. It isn't everybody who knows an author. Cupar, darling, this is the famous Colin Palgrave I've often talked about.'

'My second book is not quite ready yet,' said Palgrave, forcing himself to adopt a light tone. 'As a matter of fact,' he went on, addressing Miranda, 'I've had all I can use, I think, in this place, so I'm moving on tomorrow. Actually I'm clearing out tonight, so you two – ' he smiled at the married couple – 'couldn't have come at a better time if you want to take up your option.'

'Oh, dear!' said Morag, her face falling. (She was prettier than Palgrave had remembered.) 'Don't say we're turning you out!'

'We can surely fix up something for a day or two,' said her husband.

'No, honestly, it's all right. I've already settled for a room in a pub at Stack Ferry. I was over there today and liked the place. Besides, now that my basic theme is settled, I need to be on my own to get the book finished.'

'But what about tonight?' asked Miranda.

'Not to worry. I shall be all right. Why don't we all go to the pub and get matily bottled? The drinks are on me. We'll have a farewell party.'

But, the impromptu party over, and himself uncomfortably settled with a rug on the back seat of his car, he wished he had not been quite so precipitate in refusing the offer of the second bed in Camilla's room. If she had shown an embarrassing desire for his company, well, he had dealt drastically enough with that situation twice before, so he supposed he could have dealt with it again — 'if she dared to try it on, the little tramp,' he told himself, pulling the car rug around him and trying, for perhaps the twentieth time, a slighly rearranged position on the back seat.

With an attempt to fill his mind with something other than his own bodily discomfort, he began to think about Morag, but found neither ease nor pleasure in his thoughts. What right, he asked himself, had she to marry somebody other than himself and then to look so happy and relaxed about it? What right had she to look so much prettier, her dark hair silkier and more shining, her eyes deeper and more lustrous, her mouth more tender and alluring than ever he could remember any of these disturbing things? She had not been like this when she was supposed to be in love with him. In fact, he had often been discomfited by her tough, uncompromising outlook.

His thoughts became intolerable. He cast the inadequate car rug aside, put his shoes on, opened the car door and got out on to the road. The moon was up, the sky was clear, there was a night wind blowing across the marshes. He remembered Camilla's urge to swim by moonlight. 'Right on the broad lovely track of it, and I could swim for ever and ever,' she had said to him once. 'Moonlight on the sea makes me crazy. I could *die* for the sheer, crazy joy of being drowned in it.'

As though the memory of the girl's wild words had conjured up the girl herself, there she was, actually walking towards him along the deserted road.

'I guessed what you were going to do when Adrian told me you had taken them for a farewell party,' she said, coming up. 'Guess what *I'm* going to do.'

Palgrave laughed.

'Ill met by moonlight, proud Titania,' he said. 'I suppose you're going swimming.'

'Come with me, do! It's warmer in the sea than out of it, once the sun goes in.'

'Oh, all right,' he said. 'It will help to get through a bit of the night. It's damned uncomfortable and draughty in the car. One has to leave a window open to let some air in, and I've nothing to cover me up except one small rug that's only meant to go over my passenger's knees.'

'Well, poor old Colin had the chance of something better, I expect, and turned it down,' she said mockingly. 'Afraid for his precious virtue, was he?'

'No. He just doesn't go to bed with schoolgirls, as I've told you before.' By this time they were on the causeway which led across the marshes. The moonlight made everything unreal. The dunes, in the distance, were black and silver; the creek was full of stranger and lovelier light than the sun's rays ever discovered; the distant sea, which, to Palgrave, had seemed almost silent by day, had now found an eerie voice and, as they approached it, a luminosity apart from the flooding moonlight, for every creaming little wave was tipped with silver as the incoming tide lazily tossed it on to the shore and then gently but inexorably pulled it back again.

Camilla slipped off her jeans and sweater and ran across the sand. Palgrave undressed more slowly, shivering as the night wind made its first impact upon his naked body. Then he too ran across the strip of muddy beach and splashed his way to water deep enough for swimming. As he warmed up, he began to enjoy himself.

'Swim *with* me!' Camilla called out. 'You be the dolphin and I'll be the boy on your back.'

He swam over to her, put his hand on her head and thrust her under. When she surfaced, laughing and pushing the hair out of her eyes, he asked, coming behind her, taking her by the elbows and towing her along on her back:

'Is that the game you were playing with the boyfriend the other morning?'

'What other morning?'

'No, it couldn't have been. You were paddling and skylarking, not swimming. The tide was going out.'

'How do *you* know anything about it?'

' "My name is Ozymandias, king of kings." '

'Oh, don't come the little schoolmaster over me! Catch me if you can!' She freed herself from him by suddenly sitting up, for he was not so much grasping her elbows as supporting them. As he was about to retort, for he felt the implied contempt in her remark, he went under and came up choking. He soon recovered and after another short, fast burst out to sea, he splashed ashore, dried himself on his shirt, put on the rest of his clothes and floundered his way across the marshes, leaving the girl still in the water.

When he reached the road the thought of spending the rest of the night in the car, cramped, uncomfortable and cold – for now he lacked even his shirt, which was too damp to put on – made him think longingly of that other bed in Camilla's room. In any case, his suitcase was still in the cottage. It would supply him with a dry shirt. He would have plenty of time to nip indoors and put on the clean shirt, whether, in the end, he slept in the bed or not.

Miranda had given him a key to the front door of the cottage and, a Londoner and so accustomed to take such precautions, he had always locked the front door before he went to bed. He assumed that the newcomers would do the same. He had the key in his trousers pocket, so he entered as noiselessly as he could and groped for his suitcase, but it had been moved to make room for the luggage of the new tenants and it took him a few moments to find out where it had been placed.

He located it stealthily at last, picked it up and crept up the stairs and into Camilla's room. Here he took off and packed the things he was wearing and put on a suit and a smarter pair of shoes. To do all this he had to put on the light and he was wryly amused to note that Camilla, in what he supposed had been a hopeful spirit, must have pulled the two single beds close together so that they looked like a double.

The temptation to get into one of the beds and sleep was strong. He even reached the stage of pulling the beds apart and flinging back the covers of the one nearer the door, but recognising immediately the compromising nature of this policy if he intended to keep the persistent nymph out of his arms, he put the temptation aside, took a look at himself in the fly-blown mirror over the dressing-table and decided that he needed a shave and that there might be no other opportunity for this before he presented himself at the hotel in Stack Ferry and asked whether he might take up his option earlier than had been arranged.

He crept down the steep stairs and went into the kitchen. Here he heated some water, took off his jacket, shaved, patted on some aftershave lotion, repacked the suitcase whose contents he had had to disarrange and then, picking up the suitcase once more, he stole into the sitting-room and went towards the front door.

This time he saw that a shaft of moonlight had fallen across the studio couch. It picked out a man's bare arm lying outside the coverlet and across a stubbled cheek and stiff red hair.

'Must be a sound sleeper, especially for a doctor,' thought Palgrave. 'Surely my groping around for my suitcase when I first came in ought to have woken him up?' Of Morag there was no sign. Palgrave supposed that she was taking a moonlight stroll. The moon had always fascinated her, he remembered, and during the months of their engagement he had remonstrated with her more than once about her moonlit walks and the possible danger of taking them alone. She had never given way, he remembered.

Palgrave stood looking down on the sleeping man, the man who now slept nightly with Palgrave's woman. Turbulent thoughts and crazy fantasies passed through the watcher's mind. Suppose that Cupar died? Suppose there was a rail crash or a street accident? Suppose a gang of murderous young thugs set upon him and killed him? If Cupar ceased to exist, perhaps Morag would turn to Palgrave for comfort and from comfort to love and from love to marriage. His wild thoughts ran away with him.

'And there's my book!' Palgrave suddenly said aloud. 'I didn't intend to write a thriller, and I shan't. This will be a psychological novel of sex and violent death. Eureka! I really believe I have it!'

Because he had said the words aloud, he disturbed the sleeping man. Cupar snorted, rolled over and opened his eyes. Palgrave retreated into the shadows and waited for the other to settle down again. Then he made for the door and, baggage in hand, sneaked out without actually latching the door behind him. Morag and Camilla would be returning sooner or later, he supposed. He half wondered whether he would meet Morag on the road, for he had given up all intention of trying to sleep in his car. The road, however, was deserted and there was nothing moving on the marshes except the tall plants along the shores of the creek. They were swaying and whispering in the moonlight and seemed to be dancing to the soundless music of a gentle but persistent off-shore wind.

Palgrave walked to his car, put his luggage in the boot and took the driver's seat. He fastened his seat-belt and decided to drive westwards along the coast road. There was nobody about. Morag, if she was out walking, must have gone in the opposite direction, he supposed, or else she was out on the marshes or among the dunes. Possibly she, too, had gone for a swim.

There was no sign of Camilla, either, but this was not surprising. Both the dunes and the pebble-ridge would hide her from his seat in the low-slung car, whether she was still in the water or not. He did not suppose she was still swimming. The tide had been nearly at the full. Either it was slack water by this time, or else the tide was on the turn. She surely would be out of the water by now. He half thought of leaving the car and going down to the beach to make certain of this, but just as he was about to unfasten his seat-belt, he saw what he took to be Morag. She had been wearing white trousers and a white cardigan at the farewell party, and it was a white form which appeared in the distance flitting over the marshes.

'Must be a will o' the wisp,' he thought, 'Gases rise over marshes. I shall have to put Morag out of my mind. Curse young Camilla and her sexy urges!' He let in the clutch and drove in the moonlight towards Stack Ferry.

CHAPTER 5

THE DEAD

'In your deep floods
Drown all my faults and fears.'
Phineas Fletcher

He drove west and then south, found, in the early morning, a lorry-drivers' café, breakfasted on delicious ham and eggs and execrable coffee, and then set course north and east for Stack Ferry. His chosen inn, The Stadholder, had its own courtyard. He drove in under an archway, locked the car and went off to kill time before presenting himself at the reception desk to ask whether he might move in straight away instead of waiting until Saturday.

The marshes of Stack Ferry stretched away north of the town itself, and both east and west of the estuary. Those to the west had been drained and grass-sown, for they were freshwater marshes, and were now turned into a public park and a caravan site. Palgrave explored them, but found them uninteresting. Beyond the park, however, the marshes were as Nature had intended them to be.

Those on the east side were sea-marshes, but, unlike the stretches at Saltacres, these at Stack Ferry were boggy and so much intersected by ditches, channels and little creeks and inlets as to be impassable except to wild-fowlers in punts. Palgrave walked a couple of miles back along the road towards Saltacres and then took a path which led seawards, but at the end of a mile or so the path petered out and he found his way blocked by a creek which meandered through the marshes and was too wide to jump across.

At half past eleven he presented himself at the inn and was told that he could settle in and that his room would be ready for him after lunch. He spent the day quietly, thinking about his book, and on the following morning he was in the bar finishing his first pint when Adrian walked in. Palgrave had told him where he would be staying and had been expecting that he and Miranda would at least telephone him before they returned to London, but he had not thought to see either of them because they had no transport. Adrian, however, had not come merely to see him, but to make a pertinent enquiry.

'I'm not really worried,' he said, 'but it seems an extraordinary thing for even Camilla to do, don't you think?'

'What does?'

'To sling her hook without a word to Miranda or me. She hasn't by any chance thrown in her lot with you, I suppose? I've walked all the way over to ask you. Is she here?'

'Good gracious, no! I should soon give her the bird if she showed any signs of trying to team up. Surely you know that! What, exactly, has happened?'

'That's what we don't know. We heard her go out the night before last and assumed she'd gone for a swim. She was a great one for moonlight bathing.'

'I know. As a matter of fact, I went bathing with her the night I left Saltacres. Oh, not by arrangement. I was intending to spend the night in my car, but I was cramped and cold, so I got out to stretch my legs and do a few exercises to warm myself up a bit, when along comes the wretched girl and suggests this moonlight swim.'

'You went down to the sands with her?'

'I did, and into the water. I didn't stay in long and I left her there. That is the last I've seen of her.'

'Did she mention anything about her plans? It's quite a long walk to the sea across the marshes. You must have talked as you walked from your car to the beach.'

'I suppose we chatted, but I can't remember what we talked about. Certainly no mention was made of any plans. I didn't even tell her mine.'

'All Miranda and I could think was that Camilla felt Cupar and his wife had turned you out, and that she was resentful about it. But you say she has made no attempt to join you here. We thought at first that she had slipped out early yesterday morning, but we've seen nothing of her at all.'

'The last I saw of her, I tell you, was in the water. I soon had enough of moonlight bathing, so I left her to it, and that's all I know. I shouldn't worry about her, if I were you. I expect you're right and she's taken a scunner at the other two. I'll tell you, Adrian, why I oiled out. It's because I was once engaged to Morag and that made too much of an awkwardness if we were under the same roof, particularly as it was I who broke the engagement.'

'If I may ask, why did you? She seems a charming woman, very pretty, too.'

'Yes. I was a fool. I knew I'd been a fool when I met her again the other day. I thought marriage would interfere with my writing and that I'd be tied to schoolmastering all my life just to support a wife and family. That's why I turned her down. I bitterly regret it now.'

'Oh, but I quite understand. One's work must come first. But, Colin, what are we to do about that girl?'

'Are you sure that Camilla really has left the cottage? She isn't just out on the spree again?'

'We don't think so. She's taken her suitcase and all her clothes have gone.'

'Yes, that does look a bit final. Now, let me buy you a drink, and then I'll give you a lift back to the cottage. Not to worry about her. She knows how to look after herself,' said Palgrave.

That afternoon he sat on the bed in his little room, writing pad on knee, and made more notes for the book which at last showed signs of life. The notes were copious and his pose uncomfortable, but something was definitely taking shape and by tea-time, when he went in search of a café (The Stadholder did not serve teas) he was well content with the progress he had made and decided to let the yeast work for the next couple of days before he began the actual writing of the book.

During the next two days he explored the countryside by car and tried to put Morag out of his mind. He found the magnificent ruins of William d'Albini's massive Norman keep, and, later, the beautiful, impressive remains of a Cluniac priory. These things would go into the book, he decided.

On the Friday, with no very definite plans for the day, he breakfasted later than usual and then strolled out to buy a newspaper. There was an item of news in it which affected him so deeply that he read it three times before he could believe that it was there.

He put the paper down and stared at the wall without being conscious of seeing it. What he saw was a wild-haired girl in a sweater which looked much too roomy and long for her, washed-out blue jeans which came halfway down her sun-browned calves, her bright, eager young face, vivacious but not really pretty, her muddy shoes, and then he heard a clear voice which had come to him on an off-shore breeze and which had cheerfully called out, 'Hi!'

The newspaper report was short, but it was at the bottom of the front page, otherwise (for he was not a man to read a paper assiduously) he might have missed it. It stated that a body washed up on the shore near the village of Saltacres had been identified as that of Miss Camilla Hoveton St John, a summer visitor from London. Foul play was not suspected.

When he had assimilated this laconic information, Palgrave went out to get a copy of the local paper. This had a longer and more detailed account. Camilla, it stated, was thought to have bathed on an outgoing tide and drowned in a vain effort to reach the shore. Bathing along that part of the coast was safe enough when the tide was right and Miss St John was said to have been a capable swimmer, but she liked to bathe at night and must have mistaken the state of the tide or trusted too much in her own strength and skill. Fatalities had occurred before in that neighbourhood, but visitors were usually warned by local boatmen, or other residents, of the dangers of a powerful undertow, and there was evidence that this had been done in the present case. By day a swimmer in difficulties might be able to attract attention from a passing yacht or somebody on shore, but at night this was unlikely, nor would the hoisting of a danger cone or other warning device have been effective under the circumstances. Few people bathed alone on that part of the coast, even by daylight. To bathe alone at night was asking for trouble. Moreover, there was more than a mile to walk from the village to the sea. However, Miss St John was accustomed to bathe alone, but, most unfortunately, had done so once too often.

Palgrave got out his car and drove eastwards to Saltacres and the holiday cottage. Miranda, her plump, usually happy face clouded with shock and grief, and Adrian, haggard and with his cheeks fallen in, were alone. If he could be glad of anything at such a time, Palgrave was glad of this.

'The inquest is to be on Monday, at Stack Ferry,' said Miranda. 'We were to have gone home, but of course we must stay up for it. Will you be there, Colin?'

'Yes, of course. Will you tell me all that has happened?'

'But we know nothing of what has happened, except that poor little Camilla is dead. We can't believe it *has* happened. She was so young, so vital, such a good swimmer. She had this *thing,* if you remember, of bathing at night. She thought it was romantic.'

'But she bathed in the daytime, too. I've been in with her once or twice, and so has at least one other chap. I've seen them together.'

'I suppose there was nothing much else for her to do here but bathe and wander about. We brought her because we thought she might like to paint scenery that was new to her, but she has done very little work down here.'

'By the way, what has happened to the Lowsons?'

'Cupar and Morag? Oh, they hired a boat and a boatman and have gone sailing. They are kind people and thought we would prefer to be by ourselves for a bit. Not much fun for them, anyway, with us so concerned and sad, and visits from the police and all that,' said Miranda.

'Oh, the police have been here, have they?'

'But of course. They asked all sorts of questions. It could be a case of suicide, you see.'

'But nothing worse?'

'Oh, Colin, of course not!'

'What questions did they ask?'

'Oh, whether she was accustomed to bathe alone.'

'Was my name mentioned?'

'Of course.'

'Do they know we bathed together the night before I went to Stack Ferry?'

'We told them that, because you had told Adrian you did, but that you had gone to Stack Ferry and could know nothing about her death. The fact that she came back here and packed her suitcase and took it away proves that she could not have been drowned that night.'

'Has the suitcase been found? The report in the newspaper – the local paper – said nothing about it. Have the police traced it, I wonder?'

'We know nothing about the suitcase. She must have found other lodgings and the suitcase will turn up there. But there is nowhere in the village where she could stay.'

'She must have been shacking up with some man, don't you think? One of the summer visitors who had rented a cottage?'

'That *is* what we wondered, too. You know what she was like.'

'Somebody she met that day she took my car, perhaps, or the chap I saw her with once. If that is so, ten to one the chap won't be too anxious to come forward.'

'Why not? The death was an accident.'

'What else did the police want to know?'

'Only whether she was happy or had anything on her mind. Well, of course, if she had anything on her mind, it was men, but we did not tell them that.'

'Why not?'

'Well, but, Colin, the poor child is dead! We couldn't put her in a bad light *now*!'

'Are the police likely to come here again?'

'I shouldn't think so,' said Adrian, speaking for the first time during the interview. 'I suppose it depends on what comes out at the inquest. I just simply hope nothing does.'

'How do you mean?'

'Nothing will ever convince me that Camilla swam when the tide was going out. Even by night she'd have known what it was doing, which way it was running. She knew all about the dangers of this part of the coast and, besides, she had a manual of tide-tables.'

'I suppose—' began Miranda.

'Yes?'

'Well, you know how fond she was of you, Colin.'

'Fond of me, my foot! I was just another man to be pursued, that's all. If you're suggesting that she came after me to Stack Ferry and oiled herself in at The Stadholder, well, simply, she didn't. She didn't even know where I was staying, did she?'

'She could have asked around until she found you,' said Adrian.

'She never came anywhere near me at Stack Ferry. What if she *had* done? She wasn't drowned there. The tide sets the wrong way for that. She would have been carried – oh, no, perhaps she wouldn't though. Anyway, whether she came to Stack Ferry or not, I certainly saw nothing of her there.' He realised, too late, that he was on the defensive and that Adrian knew it.

'Not to worry, Colin,' he said kindly. 'The police seem satisfied that she bathed alone on an outgoing tide and at night. That will be the end of the matter. I'm glad she had no parents. I hate breaking bad news.'

The inquest was soon over. Adrian went through the formality of identifying the body and the medical evidence of death by drowning was clear. There was only one unsatisfactory detail, but on this neither the police surgeon nor the pathologist was prepared to be dogmatic. Neither would commit himself as to the exact time of death to within a period of forty-eight hours. The body had been some time in the water, so the usual rate of decomposition had been retarded. There was more explanation given, but perhaps the most important feature, so far as the police and the public were concerned, was that there were no marks of violence on the body and no evidence that the deceased had been other than a completely healthy and carefree young woman who, although she was not a virgin, was not pregnant.

The verdict (to quote the local paper) was a foregone conclusion. The deceased had come by her death accidentally through drowning on an outgoing tide. The coroner pontificated upon this for the benefit of other holidaymakers and the incident appeared to be closed. Palgrave attended the inquest but not the funeral. He returned to Stack Ferry and suddenly found the opening sentences for his book.

He was not quite so lucky in dismissing Camilla from his mind as he had hoped to be. Apparently Adrian and Miranda were not the only people who were puzzled by the disappearance of Camilla's suitcase. He had been back to The Stadholder for a couple of days when there came a tap at his bedroom door.

'Telephone, Mr. Palgrave.'

'Oh, thanks.' It must be from the Kirbys, he supposed. He wondered what Adrian or Miranda had to tell him. He assumed that they had returned to London as soon as the funeral was over. However, it was neither of them on the line.

'Mr Palgrave?'

'Speaking.'

'County Police here, sir. We'd like a word with you.'

'I'm not in trouble about my car, I hope?'

'Nothing like that, sir. We think you may be able to give us a little help over another matter. Would you prefer us to come to you, or would you rather come to the station?'

'What's it all about?'

'I would rather not talk over the telephone, sir.'

'Oh, in that case, you had better come here, then. When can I expect you?'

'Would noon tomorrow suit you, sir?'

'Oh, yes, I suppose so, but I wish I knew what it was all about.'

'Until tomorrow then, sir, at noon. I shall be in plain clothes, of course.'

Like most law-abiding people, Palgrave was happy enough to know that a police force, however greatly undermanned it might be, did at least exist, but, again like the majority of citizens, he was much less happy when a member of it looked him up personally and began asking questions.

'You will have heard about the drowning fatality, sir? We believe you were intimate with the dead girl. I refer to your relationship with the late Miss Hoveton St John.'

'I don't care for your use of the word "intimate", Inspector. It conveys an entirely false representation of my relationship with Miss Hoveton St John.'

'So there was a relationship, sir?'

'She was a holiday acquaintance, that's all.'

'But you stayed at the same cottage as she did, I believe. Wasn't that so?'

'I was there for a few days before I moved to this hotel, yes.'

'Why did you move on, sir?'

'The cottage became overcrowded. Two more people turned up, so I opted out.'

'You did not move because the young lady had become an embarrassment to you?'

'Good heavens, no! It was just to make room for the newcomers.'

'Had they the prior claim, then?'

'Well, actually, I suppose not. It was a case of an overbooking.'

'Then what made you decide to leave? I am told that arrangements had been made to accommodate you.'

'Look, Inspector, what *is* all this, for goodness' sake? The "arrangements" you mention were most unsatisfactory. Why shouldn't I have moved on?'

'*I'll* ask the questions, if you don't mind, sir. *Why* did you leave Saltacres so precipitately?'

'I've told you. There's nothing else I can say.'

'Would you mind if I had a look round your bedroom, sir?' (They were in a corner of the bar.)

'Good Lord! Why? I'm not a dope smuggler, neither have I half a dozen illegal immigrants hidden under the bed!'

'If I might just have a look round, sir.'

Palgrave produced his key. The Inspector was not long gone. He handed back the key. Palgrave took it with an attempt at a contemptuous snort.

'I hope you found the hoard of illicit diamonds,' he said.

'Now, now, sir,' said the Inspector, smoothly. 'All I was looking for was a suitcase.'

'Well, you were in luck, then, weren't you? I actually possess such an object. I hope you examined it for a false bottom.'

The Inspector smiled gently.

'I am perfectly satisfied with what I found, sir – or, rather, with what I did *not* find.'

'And that was? – or shall I be snubbed again for daring to ask a question?'

'We are still looking for the suitcase which belonged to the deceased. Thank you for your co-operation, sir. I don't think I shall need to trouble you again.'

'That's as well. I shall be leaving here quite soon and going back to London. No objection to that, I hope? Do you want my home address?'

'That will not be necessary, sir,' said the Inspector gravely.

'We have all the information we need at present. Is it true that you went swimming with the young lady?'

'Now and again I did.'

'When was the last time, sir?'

'The night before I came here. Why?'

'Just cross-checking, sir. You mean that you were the last of your party to see her alive.'

'How do you know that? I was not the only one from the cottage who was out that night.'

'Your exit disturbed the gentleman in the parlour. What made you return to the premises that night, sir?'

'I went back to collect my things.'

'Would that not have waited until the morning?'

'I suppose so, but I thought I might as well be off.'

'And where was the young lady, when you returned to collect your things?'

'Still in the sea, I suppose. She always stayed in the water much longer than I did.'

'Were any other members of your party out that night, sir?'

'We all were, at some time or other. When I found myself unwilling to accept the arrangements which had been made to accommodate us all, I took the entire party out for a farewell drink. I didn't want anybody to think I was going off in a huff. It was none of their faults that the cottage had been double-booked.'

'Was Miss St John with you?'

'No. She wasn't in the cottage when I issued my invitation and, to save you the bother of asking the question, I have no idea where she was.'

'But you met her later.'

'Purely by accident. I was standing beside my car when she came along and asked me to come for a swim. It was so damned uncomfortable trying to sleep in the car that I thought I might as well use up some of the time, so I went along with her. I came out of the water before she did, dried and dressed, went back to the cottage to change my clothes, as I think I told you, collected my suitcase and drove about until I found a café where I could get some breakfast.'

'After you had had your drinks, sir, can you be sure that the rest of your party returned to the cottage?'

'No, of course I can't be sure. My car was parked further up the road. I said goodbye, climbed into it and made myself as comfortable as I could on the back seat.'

'And later you went swimming with Miss St John.'

'That's the size of it.'

'Did either of you see anybody else about?'

Palgrave thought for a moment in order to consider his answer.

'I believe one or two of the others may have gone for a stroll by moonlight,' he said, 'but I couldn't be sure. There was some talk of it, I believe.'

'While you were at the public house?'

'Yes, that's when it would have been.'

'But you don't know whether any of the party except you and Miss St John were actually out of the cottage while you were swimming?'

Palgrave could answer that question truthfully and without equivocation.

'No,' he said. 'I know nothing of what the others were doing while we were swimming.'

'What about when you went back to the cottage after your bathe?'

'I've no idea about that, either.' The Inspector gave him a very sharp glance, but did not query the answer. He closed his notebook and merely said:

'Thank you for your help, sir. It's only the missing suitcase that bothers us. Mr and Mrs Kirby, who brought the young lady down here on holiday, are convinced that she wouldn't have bathed on an outgoing tide. Have you any ideas about that, sir?'

'She wouldn't if she had *realised* that the tide was going out.'

'Just so, sir. If she had *realised*. Just so.'

CHAPTER 6

SERIOUS DOUBTS

'Ah, salt and sterile as her kisses were,
The wild sea winds her and the green gulfs bear
Hither and thither, and vex and work her wrong,
Blind gods that cannot spare.'

A.C. Swinburne

Somewhat shattered by the interview with the Inspector, Palgrave decided to leave Stack Ferry at the end of the week. The plot of his book was maturing in the most irresistible and comforting way. All that remained, he thought, was to write the story. That would be done more conveniently in his London lodgings than in the claustrophobic, barely furnished little upstair room at The Stadholder, especially if it was going to be open to police inspection at any hour of the day or night.

He recognised this last thought as psychotic and wondered whether he was becoming the victim of a persecution mania. This must at all costs be suppressed. He could not afford to have irrational fears come between him and his novel.

He thought he had settled upon his heroine. She was to be a *femme fatale* in her early thirties, beautiful, sophisticated, incredibly attractive, but he realised that she was turning into Morag, and this was the last thing he had either envisaged or wanted. He made a determined effort to turn her into the Camilla he had known. She would have to be older than Camilla, of course, and that coltish immaturity changed to suit his theme, but Camilla it would have to be. In bed that night he wondered (and found himself worried about it) whether in death she was going to haunt him even more effectively than, during the few days of their acquaintanceship, she had attempted to do in life.

He began to think over everything he knew about Camilla.

It was precious little, but that, he realised, would prove more of an advantage than the reverse. She would have to be provided with a background. He wondered what sort of childhood she had had, how and when she had lost both her parents and under whose testamentary dispositions she had obtained her modest but undeniable private income.

He knew that she had shared a London flat with three other women all older than herself. He had heard little about them from Camilla, but Miranda had told him more. There was fat, dark, slightly moustached Gerda who, like Miranda, taught part-time at the art school and otherwise painted racehorses, pedigree hunters and showy little trotting-ponies. There was Mevagissey, descendant, (according to Camilla, who obviously had not believed the claim) of a hundred earls and was now in her fifth year at the art school because she had set her cap at the principal and was still hoping to trap him into marrying her. Lastly there was Fenella, who, according to Camilla, was a callgirl when she was not at the art school where, so far, she had not learnt enough even to slap paint on a barn door, let alone contrive a decent picture.

He wondered how soon they had learned of Camilla's death. Miranda would have told them by this time, even if they had not read of it in the papers. He wondered how they had taken the news. Had they been fond of Camilla, he wondered, or had they regarded her merely as a person who was good for her share of the rent? He began weaving fantasies which became wilder and more unlikely as sleep came nearer to him. When he did fall asleep, his dreams were even more fantastic than his thoughts and filled him with an almost nightmare dread, so that he was relieved to be awake again.

He worked hard all the next morning on his book and in the afternoon took his car out. He cruised around the neighbourhood for an hour or so, followed the road to the south and then came upon a signpost which showed that there was a cross-country route to Saltacres. He had no desire to return there, but concluded that there would be a diversion somewhere along the route which would take him back to Stack Ferry.

Then another thought struck him. Adrian and Miranda would have vacated the cottage and gone back to London, but the Lowsons would still be in possession. A longing came over him to see Morag again. When he came to a turning which would have taken him back to Stack Ferry he avoided it and continued on his way.

He was ready with his excuse for calling on the Lowsons. He would ask whether they knew the Kirbys' London address so that he could write and thank them for their kindness to him and to ask whether he might call upon them when he got back to his lodgings and take them out for a drink or perhaps to the theatre.

Thus armed, he parked his car in the wide part of the village street where he had always left it, smoothed down his hair and went along to knock on the cottage door.

Morag was alone. She did not seem in the least surprised to see him, but invited him in as though she had been expecting him.

'Why, Colin, how very nice!' she said. 'We were hoping you would call before you went back to London. Miranda was sorry you didn't go to the funeral, but Adrian said it was understandable, as you hardly knew the poor girl.'

'I knew her quite well enough, thank you!' Palgrave found himself saying.

'Oh, dear, yes, I know! Well, do sit down and I'll get the tea. I'm sorry Cupar isn't here. He's out sailing. I didn't want to go, but I'm awfully glad of some company.'

'I haven't really come to inflict myself on you,' said Palgrave. 'I just wanted Adrian's London address, if you have it.'

'Yes, I do have it, but please don't hurry away. You don't look very well, Colin. You're worried about that poor girl's death, aren't you? So are your friends, you know. They're so worried that they are going to do something about it.'

'What can anybody do? She's dead; the coroner has given the only verdict which is possible under the circumstances, and there's an end of it.'

'Your friends don't think so. I believe they're wasting their time and that of the police, but they are determined to keep the case open.'

'But, Morag, there simply isn't a case, and when you call them my friends, well, I hope they are, but I've only known them since I came down here.'

'Yes, they told me. You were a stranger and they took you in – literally, not metaphorically, of course.'

'It was really Camilla's doing, I think, although the invitation was supposed to come from them. I wish to goodness now that I'd refused it.'

'Because this drowning business has happened? My thought is that it would have happened anyway. I think the verdict was right. The poor girl chose the wrong state of the tide, got carried out to sea on an undertow, couldn't get back and was drowned. The incoming tide brought the body back to shore and somebody – that man who gave evidence at the inquest – found and reported it. It's all simple enough and it's the sort of thing that must happen every year during the holiday season on some part of the coast. People who ought to know better *will* do these daft things, and you must know, being one of them yourself, as I well remember, that there is nobody so arrogant as a strong swimmer.'

'She wasn't all that strong a swimmer,' said Palgrave. 'She wasn't nearly as powerful as you, from what I remember, but she couldn't have drowned that last night I was here. The tide was still coming in. Mind you, if later on she *did* bathe on an outgoing tide and got carried out to sea, I don't think she could have fought her way back. I had the devil of a job myself that time I was fool enough to pit myself against the undertow. It was terribly alarming and one tended to panic, which certainly didn't help matters.'

'Well, Adrian and Miranda are so certain that the girl would never have taken such a risk that, apart from anything the police may be thinking of doing, they have decided to take matters further.'

'How do you mean?'

'They want to put a private investigator on to the job of finding out what happened. It's a nuisance the doctors couldn't decide exactly when the girl was drowned and, of course, there is still the question of that suitcase of hers. It hasn't turned up anywhere yet.'

'So what exactly are Adrian and Miranda trying to do? I hope they are not taking on more than they can cope with.'

'Oh, they are going to do that, all right.'

'You mean they've got hold of some private eye who'll lead

them up the garden and charge them the earth for doing so?'

'Not at all. They are going to find out whether Dame Beatrice Lestrange Bradley will look into the thing for them.'

'But she's a top-notch mental specialist, accredited to the Home Office and goodness knows what all besides! I've heard her lecture.'

'Yes, so have Cupar and I. Cupar is a doctor and he's actually met her, and he says it's a crazy idea to approach her. He says that, if she thought the case had any interesting possibilities, she'd certainly take it on and probably charge no more than her expenses, but she won't touch it, I'm sure. Of course I wish them luck with her, but, to start with, she has as much money as anybody either needs or wants, even in these days of inflation, and unless it will advance or in any way improve her reputation, which, in all conscience, is formidable enough already, she won't be interested in an open and shut case like this one. Adrian and Miranda may have their own opinions, but they are only opinions, after all, and, as Cupar says, in face of the verdict at the inquest, worth less than nothing. Of course I feel very sorry for them, because, however illogical such an attitude may be, they will always feel in some degree responsible for this girl's death. I quite understand that, nonsense though it is. By the way, how old was she?'

'Nineteen or twenty, I think, but she seemed such a kid, all the same.'

'Granted, but she was not such a kid, as you call her, in some of the ways that matter, especially to a fairly newly married wife such as myself.'

'You don't mean she made a pass at Lowson?'

'At Cupar? Yes, indeed she did. She took him for a walk and he came back quite upset and said awful things about her.'

'I thought she was out all that day. Anyway, she was a bit of a nymphomaniac, I rather fancy.'

'Is that why you left the cottage and took a room at Stack Ferry?'

'How did you know where I'd gone? Oh, I had told Adrian and Miranda, I suppose. No, Camilla was not the reason. I wanted a setting for my second book. I had hoped to find it here, but nothing worked out, so I decided to push on and try my luck elsewhere.'

'Is that the whole story?' She met his eyes and held them.

'Well, not quite. Actually I had intended to finish the week here and squash in with the overspill until Adrian and Miranda went back to London, but, well, the personnel of the overspill forced me to change my mind.'

'I see.' Palgrave saw that she did. He looked away and said:

'Well, you must admit that the circumstances had their embarrassing aspect.'

She smiled with the sudden sweetness it gave him a pang to remember.

'Not for me,' she said. 'But, then, I'm very happy, and that makes all the difference. Besides, this is the last you will see of me. We're moving.'

'Are you *really* happy, Morag?'

'There is no need to ask, is there? And if I were not?'

'They say nobody should marry a writer.'

'Except perhaps another writer, and that is something I shall never be.'

'People who inspire writers don't need to be writers themselves.'

'Colin— '

'Well?'

'You used a key to get in that night, didn't you?'

'Which night?'

'The night Camilla must have come back later and packed her suitcase.'

'I didn't know Lowson heard me. I tried not to make any noise, but I had to find my suitcase.'

'Miranda and Cupar both heard you go out. Why did you go upstairs?'

'Simple reason. I had been trying to camp out in my car and found it very uncomfortable, so I came back here and thought I might as well stretch out on the spare bed in her room for half an hour, but I changed my mind and only changed my clothes and had a shave, then went back to the car before Camilla came in.'

'Oh, I see. Well, when she did come in she must have been quieter than you were, because nobody seems to have heard a sound. I suppose she *did* come back that night?'

'She hadn't come back by the time I left, that's all I know.

What time was it when you came back from your walk?'

'My walk?'

'I thought you went for a walk on the marshes. I half thought I saw you.'

'It couldn't have been me. I was never on the marshes that night. You must have seen a ghost!'

'I hardly think so. I don't believe in them. The thing was a good way off. I took it to be you because I remembered you were wearing white.'

'But I wasn't! I had been back to the cottage and changed into something warmer before I went out again. It turned quite chilly that evening after we left the pub.'

'Yes, I can subscribe to that! It was damned chilly on the back seat of my car with a window open to let in some air. Oh, well, it must have been a pocket of mist that I saw.'

'Colin, I'm going to ask you to tell me something in confidence.'

'That sounds sinister — or it would do, if my blameless past wasn't an open book.'

'I'm not so sure about that! Anyway, here goes — and, if you refuse to answer, this jury will find you guilty.'

'You make me feel guilty already! Why are you being so mysterious?'

'Oh, there isn't any mystery. Colin, you know Camilla's suitcase and all her clothes are missing, don't you?'

'I ought to, considering that one of the County plainclothes flatties did his best to turn me and my hotel bedroom upside down in a search for the same suitcase.'

'Well, did you?'

'Did I what?'

'Sneak back here that night and pack it and take it and her off somewhere?'

Palgrave was too much astonished to be angry.

'Of course I didn't,' he said. 'What a question! The girl was far too much of an incubus for me to have taken on her and her blasted suitcase.'

'I only asked because, when you left, Miranda saw you from her bedroom window and you were carrying something.'

'Yes, my own suitcase.'

'Surely that could have waited until the morning?'

'Not if you knew how cold and uncomfortable it was, trying to kip down on the back seat of the car.'

'Anyway, I thought I remembered you putting your suitcase in the boot of your car when we were on the way to the pub.'

'Then your memory was playing tricks, my dear girl. I had every intention of coming back here to breakfast and picking up my suitcase then. It was only the discomfort of sleeping in the car that made me change my mind. Either Camilla took her suitcase out of the cottage before we had our swim, or she sneaked back after I'd gone, picked it up and went along to meet some bloke.'

'I suppose either is possible. We don't *know* there was a bloke, though, do we?'

'Oh, Morag,' said Palgrave, exasperated at last, 'don't talk so bloody daft! Of course there was a bloke, and he's not damn well going to come forward and produce that suitcase. *I* wouldn't, either, in his shoes. One thing I *do* know. Camilla would never have gone off on her own! It's true we can't *prove* there was a bloke, but, if you knew Camilla as we knew her, the inference is obvious. Besides, you said you did know.'

'You said she *sneaked* back. Why would she need to do that? She could have told Adrian and Miranda that she had changed her plans. She wasn't scared of them, was she?'

'No, but it was ungrateful to push off with somebody else when they'd brought her here with them. She may have felt delicate about leaving.'

'That doesn't sound like her. I shouldn't think she ever considered anybody but herself. If it had been known *she* was leaving, there would have been no need for *you* to go, would there?'

'Oh, Morag! Of course I had to go. You, of all people, ought to realise that! You *do* realise it! You've admitted as much.'

'Bygones have to be bygones, Colin.'

'Oh, God! Don't I know it! Well, I had better push off.'

'No, do stay for a cup of tea. I'll get it at once.' She went out to the kitchen. Palgrave walked over to the window and gazed out over the marshes. It seemed to him that an age had passed since he had seen them first. He was still standing there when Morag came in with the tea-tray.

'A penny for them!' she said gaily as she set the tray down. Palgrave turned a startled face to her.

'Good Lord! Don't say that!' he said.

'Why ever not? Oh, I see! *She* said that to you at some time or another. I'm sorry, Colin. How was I to know? Were you a little bit fond of her?'

'No, I was *not!* She was a thundering little nuisance. She latched on to me the minute she saw me.'

'Poor old Colin! Milk and two lumps is it? – or have you gone in for slimming? I tried it once, but I only got depressed and I didn't seem to lose any weight whatever. Colin, what's the matter? Is it just the girl's death, or is something else bothering you?'

'There's nothing, honestly, except that, as I told you, I had a visit from the police.'

'When?'

'Yesterday, at my hotel. They seemed to think I was hiding something.'

'And were you?'

'For goodness' sake stop barking up the wrong tree!'

'It almost looks as though they are having second thoughts about the verdict at the inquest. Adrian and Miranda are *sure* there was something wrong about the girl's death. They say she *never* would have bathed on an outgoing tide. They are certain of it, as I told you. It's they who are barking up the wrong tree.'

'The only thing which was wrong about that death was that it happened at all,' said Palgrave. 'If it wasn't accidental and somebody contrived it, the place to look is into the girl's past. I don't want to say anything more against her than I've said already, but you know as well as I do that her sort are asking for trouble every minute of their waking lives.'

'If she was only about twenty years old, she couldn't have had all that much of a past, though, could she?'

'Oh, they begin at eleven years old these days. They get away with it for a time, but they're caught out in the end.'

'But not necessarily murdered.'

'Who's talking about murder?'

'I thought *we* were, because that's what Adrian and Miranda think. I think they're crazy.'

'Oh, yes, they're going much too far. As I say, she met some bloke – probably that day she pinched my car and went off with Adrian to Stack Ferry – and they met again by arrangement, probably more than once— '

'And bathed together on an outgoing tide? Then why wasn't the man drowned as well as the girl?'

'That's quite an easy one. It may have been a mere matter of muscle. *I* bathed on an outgoing tide once, as I told you, and got back all right. It was a fight, but I managed it and so, we may assume, did he. Or he may have stayed in shallow water and been in no particular danger. But what's the use of speculating?'

'No use at all. Well, if you don't want any more tea, I'll get you Adrian's address and then perhaps you had better go.'

'Thanks.' He looked at her helplessly. 'I – well, yes, I think I *had* better go.'

Morag laughed. She had always been much tougher than he, he reflected, except when he had hardened his heart and broken their engagement.

PART TWO

Dame Beatrice

CHAPTER 7

DISCREET ENQUIRIES

'Man can believe the impossible, but
man can never believe the improbable.'
Oscar Wilde

'Well, here is a thing and a very pretty thing,' said Dame Beatrice to her son who was breakfasting with her. 'A pity Laura is not here. An accomplished swimmer might be very useful in helping me to deal with this very pretty thing.' She handed a letter across the table. Sir Ferdinand studied it.

'A girl drowned by swimming on an outgoing tide?' he said. 'The writer thinks it unlikely that she would have done such a thing, but I note that he does not say it is impossible. Holidaymakers take these foolish risks, as he admits.'

'You will be leaving after lunch and Laura will not be back here for another fortnight. I am at leisure and I feel inclined to look into this matter. The writer thinks the drowned girl was involved with a man.'

'Girls always *are* involved with a man. It's what girls and men are created for. What possible interest can this particular case have for you? The writer says that the verdict at the inquest was clear and undisputed.'

'It seems to me that, although he does not say it in so many words, he suspects that the girl was murdered.'

'Well, girls on holiday are quite liable to pick up a wrong 'un, I suppose, but drowning fatalities are always a bit tricky. Very difficult to prove anything unless there is definite evidence of foul play.'

'What are you proposing to do with yourself this morning?'

'Oh, golf at Brockenhurst, I think. What time lunch?'

'When you like.'

'Let's say one-thirty, then. I'm dining this evening with

Radcliffe, so I have plenty of time. I shan't need to hurry away from here this afternoon.'

When he had left her, Dame Beatrice read Adrian Kirby's long letter again.

'We hope it is not too presumptuous of us to ask your help,' Adrian had written, 'but our lawyer told us that you were probably the only person who could get to the bottom of this mystery, for mystery it most certainly is. We are convinced, my wife and I, from all that we know of Camilla Hoveton St John, that she had far too much sense of self-preservation and ordinary commonsense, too, to have done anything so foolish as to swim on an outgoing tide on this dangerous part of the coast. We feel that if only we could trace her movements after she and her suitcase left the cottage... ' There followed several pages of explanation. Dame Beatrice perused them carefully for the third time. Then she went to the telephone, rang Adrian's number and promised to meet him at his London flat on the following day.

There was no doubt whatever about the warmth of his reply. He was more than grateful, he said, that Dame Beatrice should be willing to interest herself in the matter and that his wife would be delighted to provide her (and anybody she chose to accompany her) with a bed for the night. Dame Beatrice assured him that that would not be necessary, since her chauffeur could easily make the double journey in a day. It was then arranged that Adrian and Miranda would be ready to receive her at any time after two in the afternoon.

'Camilla was a very foolish girl,' said Miranda sadly, when the visitor had been admitted to the flat and was settled in an armchair.

'But her foolishness did not include being foolish enough to bathe on an outgoing tide,' said Adrian. 'Our friend Colin Palgrave tried it once and had great difficulty in getting back to the shore and Colin is a powerful swimmer. No, poor little Camilla died because somebody drowned her. According to the medical evidence given at the inquest, she was not a virgin. I think, therefore, that she was raped by one of the men she was in the habit of picking up, and then drowned by him so that she should not tell the tale. My main reason for wanting an enquiry, Dame Beatrice, is so that some other young girl shall not suffer the same fate at the hands of this monster. Such creatures don't stop at a solitary victim. One has only to read the papers.'

'As I understand the situation, proof of murder is going to be very difficult to come by,' said Dame Beatrice, 'unless, also as you say, the person tries again.'

'The *person*? You mean the man.'

'Not necessarily. I admit that if murder has indeed been committed, a man is the more probable suspect, but I prefer to keep an open mind. Murder by a jealous wife or fiancée is by no means unknown. You see, if you are right and murder has been committed, the likeliest thing is that Miss Hoveton St John was not drowned on an outgoing tide at all, but when the sea, as such, was perfectly safe for a swimmer. I am going on the assumption, at present, that you *are* right; that murder *has* been committed. If so, I think the body was left in the sea for the tide to turn and carry it away. If this was so, the murderer must have hoped that it would fetch up at some point on the coast a long way from Saltacres village.'

'But that,' said Miranda, 'could involve Colin Palgrave. There is no doubt he went swimming with Camilla on the night she failed to return to the cottage.'

'But she *did* return to the cottage,' said Adrian. 'She came back to collect her suitcase.'

'We don't know that she did. I think it far more likely that she went back to the cottage while the rest of us were with Colin at the pub and took it away then.'

'I can't understand what he was doing to have to go upstairs and downstairs at all. If he came back to collect his things, well, they were all in the parlour, where he had always slept until Morag and Cupar turned up,' said Adrian.

'He may have wanted to change his clothes without disturbing Morag.'

'Morag wasn't there, and he wouldn't have bothered about Cupar.'

'Do we know Morag wasn't there? – Oh, yes, of course we do. I heard her close the front door when she came back from her stroll, and that was some time after I'd seen Colin leaving.'

'How long a time?' asked Dame Beatrice.

'I couldn't say. I'd gone back to bed and I suppose I had gone to sleep. I don't think there could have been much of an interval, though.'

'Did Mrs Lowson know you had heard her come in?'

'I don't suppose so. I thought it might have been Colin back again – he had a key – '

'He wouldn't have needed it,' said Adrian. 'He told me, when I went over to Saltacres to see him after – after it happened – that he had not closed the front door behind him for fear of waking us up.'

'You thought it might have been Mr Palgrave come back,' said Dame Beatrice to Miranda. 'What made you conclude that it was Mrs Lowson?'

'First, because she closed the front door with quite a bang, whereas Colin had been very quiet, and, second, because I went to the top of the stairs and heard them – Morag and Cupar – talking. He said she had been out a long time and she said she had walked to the windmill to see it by moonlight. That was all I heard before I went back to bed.'

'Where would Mr Palgrave have gone when he went upstairs?' asked Dame Beatrice.

'Oh, into Camilla's room.'

'Which means that he knew she was not likely to come back, do you mean?'

'He certainly wouldn't have gone in if he'd known she was likely to find him there,' said Adrian. 'The wretched – sorry! – the girl absolutely haunted the poor chap – pursued him, don't you know. He was scared to death of her. I can't think why he went for that bathe.'

'However, it seems that he did and that they walked towards the sea together that night. The moon is the goddess of maidens. It is also apt to be a powerful aphrodisiac,' said Dame Beatrice.

'Oh, I expect they only went for a swim,' said Miranda. 'Colin must have found it very uncomfortable if he tried to sleep in his car.'

'I think I had better have a word with Mrs Lowson,' said Dame Beatrice.

From Adrian's description of its situation, the cottage at

Saltacres was easy enough to find and Morag was in. Dame Beatrice produced her official card.

'Oh, yes, come in,' said Morag. 'I think you have met my husband before. He will be back shortly. He has just gone into the village to get some fishing-tackle. Please sit down, Dame Beatrice. Adrian Kirby told us that he would try to get in touch with you. It is good of you to take an interest, but I don't see that there is anything anybody can do. The verdict at the inquest was quite clear and the police were satisfied with it. I know what the Kirbys think, but, after all, even the most sensible girls do foolish things at times, and I would not have called Camilla St John a sensible girl.'

'No?' said Dame Beatrice, stemming the flow of prattle and wondering why Morag was so nervous. 'Tell me what you know of her. Had you a long acquaintance with her?'

'No, indeed. She was here when we arrived, but I had never met her before and my husband and I had been here no time at all before she – before it happened.'

'Women size one another up very quickly. What did you make of her?'

'Nothing much, though I was told that she was man-mad. That sort always run into trouble sooner or later.'

'To put it bluntly, Mrs Lowson, I gather that you do not entirely dismiss what I take to be Mr Kirby's opinion.'

'That she was murdered? Oh, I can't believe *that!* The most I would say is that she met somebody the rest of us did not know, went swimming with him and that he dared her or enticed her into swimming when the tide was going out, a thing which, left to herself, she never would have done.'

'And then?'

'Well, obviously she got into difficulties and when the man found that he couldn't save her, I think he panicked and sheered off.'

'I see. What I find difficult to understand is why either of them bathed on an outgoing tide at all. Miss Hoveton St John knew the dangers and one would think that she could have convinced the man of them.'

'Girls are very silly where men are concerned, and Camilla, from what I saw of her, would have risked her life to get hold of one. Oh, here comes Cupar,' said Morag, obviously relieved.

Cupar Lowson was red-haired, rubicund, the round-faced, cherubic type to which some Lowland Scots belong. He came from Fife, he had told Dame Beatrice when they met after one of her lectures, but she decided that, far back, one of his ancestors had been numbered among the marauding Danes who had harried Northumbria and may have moved over the Border later in history.

He greeted Dame Beatrice with the utmost cordiality and reminded her that they had met in Edinburgh.

'I remember being particularly impressed by your theories as to the psychological reasons for infanticide,' he said pleasantly.

'Including infants of just under twenty-one years of age?' asked Dame Beatrice.

'Ah, you've been in touch with Adrian and Miranda Kirby. But surely they've got a bee in their bonnet?'

'That remains to be seen. However, the death of a young girl is always more of a tragedy than one can contemplate unmoved, and no doubt the Kirbys were fond of the child.'

'I don't think Adrian was,' said Morag, 'if you ask my opinion.'

'Well, at any rate, I received a most interesting letter from him. Whether he has convinced me that the girl's death was no accident is another matter entirely.'

'I don't see how any further enquiry can help clear things up,' said Lowson. 'The verdict at the inquest was clear enough.'

'I know you saw little of the girl while she was with you, but what impression did you form of her?'

'The same impression as I formed when we had her in my hospital about eighteen months ago. She had had a bit of a knock from a car – nothing very serious – and we took her in for observation, so I had a look at her as a matter of course. She tried to get on my list when I was taken into partnership by my father after I'd qualified, but I wasn't having any. I knew she'd be everlastingly in the surgery if I took her on. I told her I had got my full quota of N.H. patients and that I didn't take private cases. Both stories were lies, but I made her swallow them. I had a job to convince her. She was a very persistent young lassie. No doubt the Greeks had a word for her.'

'She was the complete man-chaser,' said Morag. 'Miranda told me about her.'

'But hardly a man-*trap*,' said her husband, grinning. 'A skinny, leggy, untidy little creature, I thought her.'

'She was a menace,' said Morag.

'She only needed some fellow who'd stand no nonsense. If such had married her, the lassie would have been well enough. He'd have made her eat regular meals, for one thing, and filled her out a bit.'

'It would be interesting to find out what happened to her suitcase,' said Dame Beatrice. 'According to something Mr Kirby mentioned in his letter to me, the police are interested in it and it seems doubtful whether Miss St John herself took it out of the cottage while the rest of you were at the public house, or whether Mr Palgrave took it. Mr Palgrave, again according to Mr Kirby, suffered some harassment from the police on this score, but they seem to have satisfied themselves that it was not in his possession. However, I shall make my own enquiries. I understand he stayed at The Stadholder in Stack Ferry.'

Dame Beatrice approved of The Stadholder – Adrian had mentioned in his letter that Palgrave had stayed there. She asked whether they could let her have a room and one for her chauffeur. As it happened, they had received a cancellation that very morning. Dame Beatrice mentioned that a young acquaintance of hers, a Mr Palgrave, had stayed at the hotel recently.

'Ah, yes, Mr Palgrave vacated his room a few days ago. Your man could have that, if agreeable to you.'

Dame Beatrice inspected the room, looked at the very narrow bed and the Spartan furnishings and made her opening gambit.

'Mr Palgrave did not have his wife with him, then,' she observed. She learned (not at all to her surprise!) that Mr Palgrave had been alone during his stay except for two men who had merely joined him in the bar. They had never set eyes on either of them before. One had slumped down as though he was very tired and from the dust on his shoes (the sharp-eyed receptionist observed) they concluded that he had walked a considerable distance. He certainly had not come by car.

As the way to the room which was now allotted to her chauffeur was reached by way of the public bar, and as, to get to the bar, the cash customers had to pass the receptionist's counter, Dame Beatrice was certain that, wherever Camilla might have gone, it was not to join Palgrave at The Stadholder. She was shown her own room, a pleasant apartment on the first floor, and reflected that the next part of her task was likely to present difficulties. It would need to be carried out in Saltacres village and the problem would be to find somebody, preferably a native of the place, who would have something to report and who would be willing to talk to her. From what she knew of the oyster-like impenetrability of the inhabitants of this particular county, especially of this northern part of it, she thought that all further proceedings would be slow ones.

For a start she spent an hour or so during the afternoon in wandering around by the Stack Ferry quay. When she returned to the hotel it was to find her chauffeur seated sedately in the entrance vestibule reading a newspaper and waiting for orders. He rose.

'George,' she said, 'could you get into conversation with a fisherman or a yachtsman and find out how the tides run on these coasts? I am wondering what happens to drowned bodies, but that need not be mentioned, although flotsam and jetsam of non-human origin would be in order as a subject of conversation. The stretch of coast I have in mind is from the bathing beach of this town round to the village of Saltacres.'

George came back with the report she had been expecting. From the Stack Ferry beach, which was to the west of the town, the tides set slantwise, coming in slightly from the west. The outgoing tide at Stack Ferry would carry flotsam round towards a village called Hallings, where the coast dipped southwards. It was impossible for anything put into the sea at Stack Ferry to fetch up at Saltacres. If it fetched up anywhere, it would be round Hallings way, and was unlikely to be washed offshore again, the outgoing tide being sluggish in those parts.

At Saltacres whatever went in on an outgoing tide was apt

to come back again on the turn. There was the story of a small yacht which had slipped its moorings and which returned to them on the next tide. Whether the tale was apocryphal or not, Dame Beatrice did not know, but it indicated that Camilla Hoveton St John probably had been drowned at Saltacres and certainly not at Stack Ferry. There remained the question of *when* she had drowned, since between a yacht which must have remained afloat and a body which, for some time, would have been submerged, there was a difference, Dame Beatrice supposed.

In his letter, however, Adrian Kirby had referred to the visit he and Camilla had made in Palgrave's car to Stack Ferry. There, in his eagerness to follow his own pursuits, he had lost track of the girl, and he had admitted that while she had been about her own devices she had most probably picked up an acquaintance who might have contacted her again at Saltacres, probably by arrangement rather than by chance.

'I think we would have known about a man at Saltacres, though,' Adrian had written, a statement which, from what she had been told about the girl, Dame Beatrice thought unduly optimistic unless some busybody had made a report which Adrian had not mentioned.

The more she thought about it, the more Dame Beatrice realised the kind of task which confronted her. If Camilla had drowned on the night when she swam with Palgrave, either her death was as accidental as the verdict at the inquest had claimed, or else Palgrave might be implicated, and very seriously implicated. That was a fact which had to be faced.

The tide-tables which she studied were not of much help, since it was not known exactly when Palgrave had given up his moonlight bathe and left Camilla still (presumably) enjoying hers. Even so little as half an hour, since they must have been swimming near enough to full tide, could have made all the difference between safe and dangerous bathing on that apparently treacherous coast.

Supposing, however, that Camilla, having removed her suitcase from the cottage while the rest of her party were enjoying Palgrave's hospitality at the inn, had met some so far unidentified acquaintance and had gone off with him, she could have been drowned, either by accident or design, at an entirely different time from that which had been supposed.

In such a case, her movements between the time Palgrave had left her, and the time of her death, would have to be traced and accounted for. Dame Beatrice went to the police, produced her credentials and asked for their help.

They were courteous, acknowledged the difficulty and agreed that there was much in what she said. They gave her an account of their own so far unavailing efforts to find the suitcase, and admitted that they themselves were no longer completely satisfied by the findings of the coroner and his jury.

'We're keeping the case open, of course, madam, and shall continue to prosecute our enquiries into the whereabouts of the missing suitcase, but that's about all we can do. If this Mr Palgrave, or the married couple he was staying with, know anything about it, they are not telling us. If she *did* go off with somebody, well, so far he hasn't come forward, and, if there is any suspicion of foul play, he isn't likely to. The chances are that the drowning happened just as the coroner indicated and that the girl herself deposited the suitcase earlier, intending to leave the cottage anyway when she knew that Mr Palgrave was determined to do so. In that case, the piece of luggage may be in some lock-up cubbyhole at the bus depôt, or in a railway station left-luggage office. Without the ticket it's going to be a long job finding it. If she was going off with a yachtsman – quite a likely thing in these parts – the suitcase could be on somebody's boat unless the owner got wind-up when he heard of the girl's death. In that case he may have dumped her bag in the sea and it could be halfway to Holland by now, if it hasn't disintegrated.'

'So much for that!' said Dame Beatrice, and thanked them. She telephoned Laura.

'Bathed in brilliant moonlight and knew about the tides?' said that accomplished swimmer. 'She wouldn't have risked it. She could have *seen* whether the sea was coming in or going out, if there was bright moonlight. No marks of violence? You wouldn't need to inflict any to drown a person in deep water. The kid was murdered. Wish I were with you!'

CHAPTER 8

TWO INTERVIEWS

'To lend our hearts and spirits wholly
To the influence of mild-minded melancholy.'
Alfred, Lord Tennyson

More to the point was the local press in the form of a young reporter from the Stack Ferry *Gazette and Advertiser*. It was this youth's practice during the summer season to make a weekly round of the hotels in the town in search of possible celebrities who might grant him an interview.

Visiting yachtsmen were his daily prey, so that his chief haunts were the saloon bars of the Stack Ferry pubs and hotels, as well as the bars down by the harbour. He was also not averse to glancing through the current entries in hotel registers when he could cajole the desk clerk (female, of course, and young) to let him take a weekly look at them.

When he saw Dame Beatrice's signature he lost no time in getting in touch with her. There came a polite tap on her door just as she was ready to go down to lunch on the third morning of her stay and a voice said:

'The *Gazette* on the telephone, Dame Beatrice.'

'And who or what is the *Gazette*?'

'The local paper, madam.'

'Ask him, her or them to call again when I've had my lunch. Two-thirty would be a convenient time.'

'Very good, madam. I'll let you know when they ring through.'

However, Dame Beatrice did not receive a telephone call, but a visit from the enterprising young man in person. They met in the lounge, which was otherwise deserted at that hour on a fine summer afternoon. He introduced himself, a self-confident but disarming, friendly youth, as Keith Dunlop.

He was accompanied by an older man who carried a camera.

'I wonder, Dame Beatrice, whether you will be kind enough to grant me an interview for my paper? I expect you get pretty bored with this kind of thing, but we'd be most awfully grateful. We don't often get people of your eminence staying in the town.'

'I always beware of flatterers, Mr Dunlop.'

'But you *will* let me talk to you, won't you?'

'There are conditions attached.'

'Don't say I mustn't quote you.'

'That was not what I meant. If I do as you wish, will you, in return, do something for me?'

'Honoured, Dame Beatrice.'

'Good. I regard that as a promise. Well, what do you want to know?'

'I've dotted down a list of questions. First, would you mind if we took a few photographs?'

'Warts and all? Oh, very well. I have seen your paper. The photography is excellent and, I hope, reliable.'

'Reliable?'

'Not so much touched up and embellished as to render the subjects unrecognisable by those who, for want of a better description (and we could well do with one) are known as the men in the street.'

Dunlop beckoned to the photographer, who was standing just inside the doorway of the lounge, and Dame Beatrice permitted herself to be photographed.

Dunlop's attendant sprite, having secured his picture, or, rather, his half-dozen pictures taken from several angles and at varying distances, then took himself and his camera away, since the interview itself held no interest for him. His last sitters had been a well-known pop group, and, after them, a psychiatrist, however eminent, was very small beer. Less well-informed than Keith Dunlop, he did not know that she was also a famous criminologist, or his views about her importance might have been different. However, he was not to be blamed. Her name seldom appeared in the newspapers as a solver of murder mysteries. Like some other famous sleuths, she preferred to leave all the credit to the police, partly, of course, for her own safety. 'Are you making a long stay,

Dame Beatrice?' asked Dunlop, creasing back a fresh page in his shorthand notebook.

'I hardly think so. I shall be here today and tomorrow. After that I may return to London for a time.'

'I thought – I looked you up, of course – I thought there was an address in Hampshire.'

'Mr Dunlop, I said I thought you could help me. I know the press are discreet. I have had reason many times to put my faith in their promises. If I tell you the reason I am here, will you undertake that not a word of it will appear openly, or by inference, innuendo, speculation or veiled suggestion, in your paper until I say the word?'

'That drowning fatality at Saltacres? I covered that, you know.'

'You are an extremely astute young man. Will you give me your promise?'

'Of course. It sounds as though you don't believe it was an accident.'

'So far, I have no idea whether it was an accident or not. I have merely been asked to make some enquiries. But, first, your questions.'

The interview followed the usual course and Dame Beatrice answered in the usual stereotyped fashion until Dunlop had worked through his list of basic questions and dotted down his last few shorthand notes.

'Thanks very much,' he said. 'that should work up into something worth while. We'll Special Feature it, with photograph, so it won't be out until next week, I'm afraid, and you may not still be here.'

'I am not sure. As I told you, it is very doubtful. My plans depend upon circumstances which are not under my control and the importance or otherwise of which I cannot, at the moment, estimate.'

'May I send a copy of the *Gazette* to your home address, then, when my article comes out?'

'It would be most kind of you.'

'The Stone House, Wandles Parva, Hampshire, isn't it?'

'Yes, that is the address, although, again as I told you, when I leave here I may be in London for a bit. But the Stone House will always find me.'

'Is the house stone-built?'

'No, it is built of mellow brick. It is called the Stone House because in its vicinity is a Stone of Sacrifice, so called.'

'*Human* sacrifice?'

'I perceive a gleam in your eye. Yes, human sacrifice, if local legend is founded on fact.'

'May I use that in my article?'

'Why not? The legend is current around my area of the New Forest.'

'Is there any story of haunted woods, sacred groves –anything of that sort?'

'Not so far as I am aware, but embroider as you will.'

'Well, that's marvellous.'

'For good measure, throw in that a distant ancestress of mine was reputed to be a witch.'

Dunlop looked at her sharp black eyes, beaky little mouth and clawlike, yellow hands and smiled.

'Maybe the ancestry wasn't all that far back,' he said, 'if what I've heard of you, both as a psychiatrist and a solver of murder mysteries, is true. Well, now, you said there was something I could do for you. I'd be glad to have a try.'

'It is something well within your scope. It concerns this death by drowning which we mentioned earlier, that of the young woman named Camilla Hoveton St John.'

'Oh, yes, I know. We covered the story pretty thoroughly and were lucky enough to get a snap of the girl which her friends took when they first got to Saltacres. Our photographer who was here a while ago blew it up and we gave it front page treatment.'

'Ah, then you know the details so far as these *are* known, and you know what conclusions were arrived at by the coroner.'

'You don't mean the verdict wasn't correct? You don't mean it was suicide? – not – I say! I *say!* You don't think it was *murder*, do you?'

'Her friends think so. For myself, I have formed no opinion up to the present. I am merely conducting an investigation on their behalf. You will say nothing about all this?'

'Dumb as an oyster, I promise you.'

'I have had it suggested to me that, on the day she spent here, Miss St John picked up some man whom she met again, without her friends' knowledge.'

'And he drowned her? Could be, I suppose. The chances are that he was one of the summer visitors, a yachtsman, perhaps. He may be anywhere by now.'

'A yachtsman? The police wondered about that. In that case, other yachtsmen may know of him.'

'What makes her friends think that the verdict on the girl was wrong?'

Dame Beatrice explained and Dunlop whistled.

'They might have something there,' he said. 'The undertow on an outgoing tide is notorious all around these coasts, but you say the girl knew about the tides and wouldn't have taken any risks.'

'I know only what I have been told.'

'Well, I'll see what I can find out. Thanks very much for seeing me and letting me in on this. Silent as the grave until you give me the all-clear.'

'Yes, silent as the grave,' said Dame Beatrice. ' "The grave's a fine and private place, but none, I think, do there embrace." '

'I beg your pardon?'

'The girl had no discretion in some matters.'

'Oh? Oh, I see. Well, there are plenty like her in this day and age.'

'How much I deplore that overworked expression!'

'Eh? Oh, me, too. One hears the words so often, though, that they trip to the tip of the tongue.'

'We are all lazy in some way or another. If we were not, people could not live with us. We should be too much for them. I myself have an intense repugnance to gardening: "When weeds, in wheels, shoot long and lovely and lush", my reaction is to let them go on doing so.'

'All the same, you're prepared to use your time and energy to do quite a bit of weeding in the case of this drowned girl. Why?'

'Curiosity. It killed the cat, Mr Dunlop, and in the end it will probably kill me.'

Dame Beatrice drove over to Saltacres on the following morning with the intention of inviting the Lowsons to lunch with her at The Stadholder. Cupar had already arranged to go sailing with a yachtsman friend, but Morag accepted the invitation with an eagerness which indicated that she was glad not to be alone for the day. As it was she and not her husband whom Dame Beatrice really wanted to talk with, the arrangements suited all parties.

Seated side by side on the back seat of Dame Beatrice's car, the two women exchanged casual chat and then Morag said,

'We had some good news by this morning's post. I don't know whether we told you that Cupar's father took him into partnership when he qualified? He died a few months ago and Cupar has now sold the practice and is going in for research, as he has always wanted to do.'

'How interesting. Research into what?'

'Heart surgery. He thinks another breakthrough is on the way, and he wants to be one of the team.'

'How interesting.'

'Yes. It means moving from London to Lancashire, but I don't mind that.'

The dining room at The Stadholder was full and in the general buzz of conversation there was little likelihood, Dame Beatrice thought, of her conversation with Morag being overheard, although she doubted whether anybody who did manage to overhear anything would make much out of it.

Morag had refused a cocktail in the lounge, so they went in fairly early to lunch and when they had ordered and the wine had been brought, Dame Beatrice abandoned polite chit-chat and settled down to business.

'Have you heard from the Kirbys?' she enquired.

'Only a short note from Miranda to say that they had been to see Camilla's flat-mates. A good thing they did, as those girls had heard nothing about her death.'

'They had not seen a newspaper report?'

'They don't read the papers much, I gather. Anyway, I expect, in the London dailies, an accidental death by drowning would only have rated a small paragraph tucked away somewhere. It's not as though the poor child was anybody important.'

'I have been interviewed by the Stack Ferry press.'

'About the drowning?'

'Well, that was not the original purpose of the interview, but I have invoked the reporter's help. He suggested that Miss Hoveton St John may have been taken for a sail in somebody's yacht on the day she came here with Mr Kirby and, at my request, the reporter is following up his own suggestion.'

'I can't see that it would help, even if somebody did take her sailing that day. It was long before she was drowned.'

'Yachtsmen belong to sailing clubs and their boats are registered with such. Yachtsmen can be traced. Whether one of them can tell me anything which will help my enquiry I do not know.'

'Dame Beatrice, you seem to be taking all this very seriously. *Do* you think Camilla was murdered? Are you saying that some crazy yachtsman took her out to sea and pushed her overboard?'

'I am saying nothing of the kind at present. I know that she met her death by drowning, but I know nothing about what happened to her beforehand.'

'I can tell you one thing, for what it's worth,' said Morag. 'It's about the suitcase.'

'Yes? You mean you know where it is?'

'No, I don't mean that.'

'It might help a great deal if we knew where she had deposited it, because we should at least know where she went when she left the cottage.'

'Well, I haven't a clue about that. All I know is what I expect people have already told you. Whenever she took her suitcase to wherever it is, she didn't leave the cottage with it on the night she went off and did not come back, and that was also the night on which Colin Palgrave left us.'

'Yes?'

'Well, I don't know how much – I mean, how many details – you've been given, but to recap, as they say, Colin didn't want to stay in the cottage after Cupar and I turned up. It wasn't just that he didn't like Miranda's rearrangement of the sleeping quarters; it was because he had once been engaged to me. He felt it was awkward our both staying in the same house. As for the broken engagement, *I* didn't mind in the least. I wouldn't have been happy if I'd married him. I know that now. Of course, I was hurt and humiliated at the time – any girl would have been – but I soon got over it and then Cupar came along.'

'A happy solution, I am sure.'

'Yes, it certainly was. It would never have done for me to have married Colin, particularly now.'

'You refer, no doubt, to the death of Miss St John.'

'Well, after Colin bathed with her that night, she was never seen alive again, was she?'

'We cannot be sure that that is so. Certainly nobody has come forward to say he saw her.'

'Please tell me something, Dame Beatrice. A woman of your eminence doesn't interest herself in a matter of this sort unless— '

'Unless she believes that something more than an accident was involved?'

'Well, yes. Was she murdered?'

'I am not the Delphic oracle, my dear.'

'And, if you were, you would give me one of its double-tongued answers, I suppose.'

'How well you understand me. Let us take a liqueur with our coffee. I must drink to our better acquaintance.'

'And then I'm afraid I must go. Cupar will be back and he likes to find me there when he gets in.' But she did not hurry, Dame Beatrice noticed. They took coffee and brandy in the lounge and their chat became desultory. Dame Beatrice thought that Morag was trying to decide whether to disclose some item of important information or whether either discretion or fear was suggesting that she remain silent on the subject she was turning over in her mind.

At last she appeared to make it up. She spoke abruptly, almost disjointedly, as she asked whether Dame Beatrice had made any enquiries at The Stadholder about Camilla's missing suitcase.

'No. I changed my mind,' Dame Beatrice said. 'Wherever the suitcase is, it is not in this hotel. I am certain of that.'

'Well, I don't believe the girl herself took it out of the cottage. In fact, I know she didn't.'

Dame Beatrice waited for more, but all Morag asked, before they left the lounge and went out to the car, was not put in a serious tone, but in a light, almost amused one which did not deceive the hearer. The question was intended seriously.

'Do you believe a murderer always returns to the scene of the crime, Dame Beatrice?'

'In my experience, a good many murderers cannot *leave* the scene of the crime without exciting suspicion,' said Dame Beatrice.

'Oh, you're speaking of domestic murders, family affairs,' said Morag. She sounded relieved.

'You began a subject you did not finish.'

'Did I?'

'It seemed so to me. How do you know that Miss St John did not take her suitcase when she left the cottage?'

'Because Cupar saw her leave the cottage while I was still out walking. He says she was carrying nothing but a towel.'

'That has little or no significance. She probably removed the suitcase from the cottage while the rest of you were at the public house.'

'I only meant that Cupar actually saw her leave the cottage.'

'That is a most important statement.' But Dame Beatrice did not disclose wherein its importance lay, or even whether she believed it.

CHAPTER 9

FURTHER INFORMATION

'One should never take sides in anything, Mr. Kelvil.'
Oscar Wilde

The next link in the chain came not from the young reporter, but from George. As she sometimes did in cases where her chauffeur's stolid air of respectability and integrity was of more use in asking questions than her own brains and acumen were likely to be, especially as, at sight of her, nervous or guilty subjects were apt to be on the defensive, she took George into partnership.

'I think you may have guessed, George, that I have been persuaded to look into the matter of a young woman who was drowned near here a short time ago.'

George, who had been cleaning the car, assumed an attentive attitude and wiped his hands on a piece of clean rag.

'Indeed, madam?'

'You have read about it?'

'The hotel staff, with whom I take my meals, showed me the local paper, madam.'

'The verdict, as you will know, therefore, was that the girl's death was accidental.'

'Due to her own foolishness in bathing at night on an outgoing tide, I understand, madam.'

'Read this letter.' She handed him Adrian's lengthy screed. When he had perused it, she said, 'You notice the date on which the writer says he accompanied the girl to this place, Stack Ferry? They spent the day here.'

'But separated almost at once, it seems, madam.'

'That is the point. He does not know where the girl went or what she did on that day, but he thinks she may have made the acquaintance of some undesirable person who followed her, and subsequently killed her, either accidentally or, as the writer believes, by his wilful act.'

'It has happened before, madam.'

'A newspaper reporter has suggested to me that the man whose acquaintance she made here – if, indeed, there was such a man – may have been a yachtsman. Now yachtsmen are a fraternity. They interest themselves in one another's boats. Will you, with your knowledge of automobile and marine engines, see whether you can find out whether there was a yachtsman involved? This may sound like what Mrs Gavin would call a tall order, but I have to begin my investigation somewhere, and what I have been able to learn from the girl's holiday companions, including the writer of this letter, has not suggested any particular line which I can follow up.'

'I shall do my best, madam. These yachtsmen are good natured, open-hearted types, on the whole. It should not be difficult to get into conversation with them.'

Realising that if George talked with yachtsmen he would also have to drink with them, Dame Beatrice did not order the car that afternoon, and it was not until she was taking a mid-morning glass of sherry on the following day that the lounge waiter told her that her man was at the reception desk to ask for orders for the day.

Rightly taking this as an intimation that George had something to tell her, she met him in the hall and they went outside to the hotel courtyard.

'You've found our yachtsman, George?'

'Yes, but I'm afraid it won't be helpful, madam. The yacht the young lady was concerned with is a family affair.'

'Oh, dear!'

'Yes, madam. There are father, mother and grown-up son. My informant thinks they took the young lady to visit the bird sanctuary out on the Point, and maybe further out to the sandbank they call Seal Island.'

'How did you come by your information?'

'The bar where yachtsmen mostly congregate was too full and too noisy for my purpose, madam. I tried it yesterday both midday and evening. This morning I hit upon what I hoped was a better idea. I went down early to the quay and hung about until I got what I had been waiting for.'

'Ah, yes, and what was that?'

'An amateur tinkering with a marine engine, madam.'

'Ah, yes, of course. I should have guessed.'

'I had to do a bit of guessing myself, madam. I thought they were in some kind of trouble — it was a biggish but old boat and a lady was standing on deck and was seemingly impatient with what was going on. Seeing me standing on the edge of the quay, she told me not to stand there, but to help her husband if there was anything I could do. I was wearing blue trousers, a white shirt and a yachting cap, madam, and I think she took me for one of the fraternity.'

'I am sure you looked the part, George.'

'I hope so, madam. I went aboard and had a look. They had had an auxiliary engine installed – a wise precaution – otherwise they were under sail. I was soon able to locate the trouble. The fault was a trifling one. All that was needed — '

'Spare me the mechanical details, George. They will be beyond my comprehension.'

'Very good, madam. Well, I got the boat under way and the old gentleman took over the controls. The lady had suggested that I accompany them in case her husband got into further difficulties, so away we went.'

'Excellent, George. And the talk turned, no doubt, to drowning fatalities along that particular coast.'

'I edged it in that direction, madam, according to your instructions, and remarked that boats were safe enough so long as they were seaworthy, but that I understood swimmers along that part of the coast were in great jeopardy if they did not pay careful attention to the state of the tide.'

'Splendid! And that, as Mrs Gavin would say, brought home the bacon?'

'The lady responded most satisfactorily, madam. The gentleman was too much occupied handling the boat to have much time for conversation.'

'I hope you were not taking undue risks in putting to sea with him, George?'

'By no means, madam. The old gentleman could handle the boat all right, the same as so many motorists can handle their cars without really knowing much about what goes on underneath the bonnet. We'd caught the tide nicely and the sea was calm. I enjoyed the trip very much, and the bird sanctuary, when we reached it, was very interesting.'

'And did the auxiliary engine fulfil its obligations?'

'We only needed it just to move off from the quay and into open water, madam. After that, we had beautiful sailing conditions and the old gentleman handled his craft with expertise, needing little help from either the lady or myself.'

'And did you learn anything in particular about Miss Hoveton St John when you referred to drowning fatalities?'

'Yes, indeed, madam, chiefly, as I said, from the lady. Having referred to the treacherous nature of the outgoing tides, I ventured the opinion that the coastguards no doubt kept an eye open for swimmers in difficulties and this led naturally to the latest drowning fatality.'

'Ah, yes. A subtle approach, George.'

'Thank you, madam. The lady was acquainted with the people who had taken Miss Hoveton St John sailing with them on the day she came here with Mr Kirby.'

'Was she, indeed? I suppose she had seen the newspaper photograph of Miss St John and recognised the face.'

'Exactly, madam. Apparently the people who had picked up Miss St John had moorings adjacent to the boat I was on, and my informant had been favoured with a good view of the young lady.'

'You speak of "people", George, and I believe you mentioned a family consisting of father, mother and grown-up son.'

'That is so, madam.'

'It does not sound very much like what I have been told about Miss St John. I should have thought a lone yachtsman would have been more to her taste.'

'My information is that Miss St John met the son in a hotel bar and he conducted her to the yacht where his parents made up a family party.'

'That must have come as an unwelcome surprise to her, I fancy.'

'So my informant seemed to think, madam, but, at any rate, off they all went. The name of the yacht is the *Juniper Mary*, and the people are called Hamilton. The yacht has left Stack Ferry, but has its own permanent moorings at a little staithe not far from Capstan Flow. The lady showed it me on the chart. I could easily find it, if you so desire.'

'I think I must pay them a visit. We will try your staithe this afternoon. In such lovely weather they may well be enjoying a cruise on their yacht, but I have noticed, George, that people who own boats seem to spend much more time at moorings than they do out at sea or in navigating rivers. I wonder at what time Miss St John was landed after her trip with these Hamiltons?'

'I asked, madam. The party came back while my informant and her husband were enjoying a cup of tea on board their own vessel, which was at moorings. She estimates that the time would have been around four-thirty and that she heard the young lady say that she must be getting back to her car. That was the last any of them – both boat parties, I mean – knew of her until they read about the drowning and saw the newspaper photograph.'

'How long will it take us to get to this staithe?'

'I can do it easily in an hour, madam.'

'Then have the car ready by two-thirty.'

They were in luck. The only person on board the yacht was a young man whom Dame Beatrice rightly assumed to be Hamilton junior. She took the bull by the horns.

'Ahoy, there, *Juniper Mary*!' she called out in her beautiful voice. The young man, who had been doing something complicated with a coil of rope, straightened himself, smiled and waved his hand.

'Coming!' he shouted and leapt down on to the tiny quay. 'What can I do for you?'

'I believe you made the acquaintance of a young woman named Camilla Hoveton St John a week or so ago, at a town called Stack Ferry, not far from here.'

'I met – *we* met – a girl called Camilla, yes. She didn't favour us with her surname. The poor kid got drowned a few days later. The local paper was full of it, complete with a blown-up photograph and a couple of columns of awful warnings to visitors about the danger of bathing on an outgoing tide. I was damn sorry to hear about it. She was a lively young specimen.'

'Her friends do not think her death was an accident. Is there anywhere that we can sit and talk?'

'Come aboard. This begins to sound interesting. Have her friends anything to go on?'

'Not enough to take to the police, but enough to satisfy themselves that more enquiries should be made. I am authorised to make those enquiries.'

'Golly! Are you a private eye, then?'

'You may call me that.' He assisted her on board, put out a deckchair for her in the cockpit and hoisted himself on to the cabin top where he sat with his long legs dangling and a look of anticipation on his youthful countenance. 'I undertook the task because I feel her friends may well be right,' she added.

'Well, she certainly didn't strike me as a girl who would easily drown.'

'What causes you to say that?'

'Oh, while my parents were looking at bird life and taking photographs, she and I sneaked off and had a swim. She was pretty useful in the water, I thought. Of course, if she was crazy enough to bathe on that outgoing tide the papers talked about, I suppose anything might have happened.'

'We do not think she bathed on an outgoing tide. She knew all about the risks there are in doing anything so foolish.'

'I say! Really? But surely that means either suicide or— '

'Yes, it does, but, of course, we have nothing much to go on, so far, so perhaps— '

'Oh, I won't breathe a syllable to a soul!'

'Why not? The more the suggestion is rumoured that the girl's death was no accident, the sooner the murderer (if there is one) will have to make a move to cover his tracks.'

'Oh, you've done this sort of sleuthing before, then?'

'A number of times, yes.' She produced her official card. 'You must not think that only Miss Hoveton St John's friends are interested in the case.'

'Christmas!' said the young man, handing back the rectangle of expensive pasteboard. 'The Home Office, eh? Big stuff, no less. Well, what do you want me to tell you? So far as I was concerned, you see, she was just a girl I picked up— '

'No, a girl who picked *you* up,' said Dame Beatrice firmly. The young man looked rueful and agreed.

'It wouldn't actually have been the other way about,' he said, 'because she really did look more than a bit of a mess.

Tatty old reach-me-downs, you know, and a gosh-awful dirty sweater far too big for her, and hair that could have done with a decent shampoo – not that one cares what people look like nowadays, of course, especially on holiday.'

'But she heard you had a yacht and thought you were alone and told you how she longed to visit the bird sanctuary but could not afford to hire a boatman or join a pleasure cruise, so— '

'Good Lord! You might have been there! Of course she hadn't banked on my parents' coming along. I could have done without them, too, of course, but I could have laughed at the expression on her face when they turned up, Ma complete with sunglasses and a tea basket and Dad in the frightful shorts he wears on the boat. Camilla looked daggers at me when they came aboard. She had shed the washed-out reach-me-downs and the dreadful sweater and was sunning herself in a bikini on the cabin top when they breezed along. She obviously hadn't expected any additions to the party, and she was anything but pleased to see them.

They weren't too delighted to see *her*, either. She was a rather obvious little sea-serpent, if it isn't disrespectful to say so. There's a type, you know, and they are not very easy to choke off. I hadn't bothered to attempt to shed her, as a matter of fact, because I knew that the parents, who are not exactly *fin de siècle* – I mean, they've *heard* of the Permissive Society, but that's about all – would soon bottle up the young lizard, and so it happened for most of the time.'

'For most of the time?'

'Well, yes. She and I went for a swim when we landed at the bird sanctuary, as I think I mentioned.'

'Did she give you any details about herself or her plans?'

'When we went swimming?'

'Or while you were all on the yacht.'

'She told my mother she was studying art and was staying in Saltacres with some people at a cottage there, that's all. Oh, she talked a lot of rot (intended to impress us, I suppose) about art being her religion, but I don't think any of us were taken in by it, and when we reached the bird sanctuary it became pretty clear that she and I were to disappear among the sand-dunes, leaving the parents to look at birds.'

'Did you find her suggestion embarrassing?'

'Not really. It struck me as damn' funny. She was so *very* undesirable. There are far better prospects at our local tennis club – and that's not saying a lot! I said it was a swim or nothing, so we swam, but not for long. She was quite good, though – a stronger swimmer than I am, as a matter of fact. I'll tell you another thing, too. She knew all about the tides along that coast. I believe her friends are right, you know. Funny she took a chance that night and got drowned. Could she have been a bit sloshed or something, and her drowning *was* accidental?'

'That is a possibility which had not occurred to me.'

'Girls can do strange things under the influence,' said young Mr Hamilton, wagging his head and looking profound.

'Men also, no doubt.'

'I once took on a bet that I'd learn to pole-vault. Chickened out later, and lost the bet, of course, after I had sobered up.'

Dame Beatrice cackled and then asked:

'What happened when you got back to Stack Ferry?'

She thanked us for a lovely outing and cut her stick. We never saw her again. I say! It's tea-time. Do come back to the house and eat a few shrimps with us.'

'May I venture to enquire whether your enterprise this day did thrive, madam?' asked George, when, seen off with smiles and cordial hand-wavings by the Hamilton family, she joined him for the return journey to Stack Ferry.

'Time will show, George. I may or may not have sown productive seed. Tomorrow we go home for the night. In Mrs Gavin's absence there will be correspondence to deal with. After that, we return to these parts to interview the house agent who lets cottages to summer visitors. Do you like this neighbourhood, George?'

'I prefer a more rolling and a more wooded countryside, madam.'

To their left stretched the miles of marshes, dunes and banks of shingle. Dame Beatrice had a sudden vision of the body of a thin young girl, her hair looking like a dark tangle of seaweed, lying dead and defenceless while the uncaring moon lit a path of glory across the sea.

'I agree with you,' she said. 'Apart from any tragedies which may have taken place in these parts, there is an infinite sadness about the landscape itself. However, so far as my researches are concerned, I make what may be called negative progress.'

'The Hamilton family were of no help, madam?'

'They were of help only in the sense that I indicate. Their son, whom I was able to interview while he was alone on the yacht, gave me his story and it was corroborated, without any prompting from him or me, by his parents, with whom, as you know, I had tea. It does not seem possible, let alone likely, that Miss St John met her murderer in Stack Ferry that day when she and Mr Kirby came there. Her time seems fully accounted for. She was alone when she met young Mr Hamilton in a bar, she was never out of sight of at least one of the Hamilton family on their trip to the bird sanctuary, she and the young man bathed and when they all returned to moorings she appears to have gone straight back to join Mr Kirby at the spot where they had parked the car. Mrs Hamilton saw them together when she, too, went ashore.'

That evening Dame Beatrice informed the receptionist at The Stadholder that she would be going home for a day and a night. She paid the hotel bill up to date and re-booked the two rooms. At the Stone House there was, as she had surmised, a pile of correspondence to be dealt with, including a long letter from Laura describing her holiday activities.

On the appointed day, George drove Dame Beatrice north-eastwards to visit the house agent who let holiday accommodation in and around the village of Saltacres. The Hamiltons had disposed of one problem. The larger matter of what had happened to Camilla's suitcase still had to be resolved.

CHAPTER 10

THE WITNESS

'I will not touch your mantle,
I'll let your clothes alone,
I'll take you out of the water clear,
My dear, to be my own.'

Anonymous

The house agent lived in a small town set among the low hills to the south of Saltacres and had only three cottages in that village on his books. One of these had been taken first by the Kirbys and then by Cupar and Morag Lowson; the second was on regular holiday hire to a family of five who booked it year after year, and the third had been let for a month that summer to a party of three young men who hired a boat and a local boatman and went fishing. Dame Beatrice ascertained that they had used up three weeks of their stay, which meant that they would have been able to see Camilla alive, had they wished to do so.

'I suppose I can book their cottage from mid-week to mid-week, Wednesday to Wednesday?' she said to the house agent. 'These men's tenancy will be up next week, you say, so if their cottage proves suitable—'

'Mid-week, madam? I am afraid the lettings are from Saturday to Saturday, on a fortnightly basis.'

'Oh, I see. Do you never deviate from that rule?'

'Not *ever*, madam, not even to oblige our regulars. It could mean leaving a cottage empty for half a week, you see, most people preferring Saturdays.'

'I quite understand. If I might have an order to view?'

She thought the three men would be back from their fishing trip and it would be too early for them to find the village pub open. She knocked on the door, therefore, at twenty minutes to six and presented the house agent's order to view.

'Oh, Lord! I'm afraid we're in an awful mess,' said the youth who had answered the door. 'We didn't reckon on clearing up until the day before we go.'

Dame Beatrice said that she quite understood and that if she might just take a quick look round she could soon satisfy herself as to whether the cottage would meet with her requirements.

'Righto. Well, if you don't mind waiting a minute, I'll see whether the other two are viewable. We rather tend to sit about in what you might call *déshabillement* these very warm evenings.' He came back after a few moments and invited her in.

The other two were in the kitchen. One took his feet off the table and both rose politely at her entrance. Dame Beatrice wished them good evening and said that she was sorry to disturb them, but if she might be permitted to look over the cottage she would be very grateful. She hardly thought it would be large enough for her requirements, as she would be bringing a party of six, including a teenage boy and girl.

'Then it won't be large enough,' said the man who appeared to be the oldest of the party and was, she judged, in his late thirties. 'There are only two bedrooms with a single bed in each, and the third one of us – well, we take it in turns to doss down on the very hard couch in the sitting-room. It's supposed to open out to make a double bed, but something's gone wrong with the works.'

'You seem to have much the same accommodation as there is in another cottage I visited and found unsuitable. In a way I am somewhat relieved, as my two youngest friends are reckless and, I'm afraid, irresponsible, and I believe there was a drowning fatality here recently.'

'Stupid girl swam on an outgoing tide. People do the daftest things when they're on holiday.'

'Did you know her?'

'Sort of. She conned us into taking her fishing one day, but fortunately – although it wasn't much fun at the time – she got most fearfully sea-sick, so that put an end to that.'

'She was an oncoming little bit of goods,' said the young man who had answered the door, 'and once she'd got her hooks into you she was as sticky as a burr.'

'Was she an attractive young girl?'

'Lord, no,' said the unchivalrous trio.

'The newspapers referred to her as a pretty brunette of twenty summers,' said Dame Beatrice. 'I suppose the drowning *was* an accident?'

'So the newspapers said. Personally, I prefer to keep an open mind. Her sort can be the hell of a nuisance when all a man wants is fishing and the pub,' said the youth who had had his feet on the table.

'Does any other holidaymaker take regular fishing-trips?'

'Not regular trips, no. As a matter of fact, most of the chaps you meet down here are yachtsmen and own their boats. They may do a bit of fishing at times. We wouldn't know.' He glanced at the others for confirmation.

'You'll excuse me for asking,' said the eldest suddenly, 'but haven't I seen you before somewhere?'

'I have no idea,' said Dame Beatrice.

'Well, I'm a solicitor. My name is Billington. I'm pretty sure I've seen you in court at some time.'

'Not in the dock, I trust.'

'No, no, of course not. Wait a minute. Didn't you appear as a witness in one of Sir Ferdinand Lestrange's cases at the Central Criminal Court a year ago?'

'It is probable. He is my son, so I am always prepared to support him.'

'That's right. He was prosecuting. Ah! I've got it. You are Dame Beatrice Lestrange Bradley and you were called to testify that the prisoner was fit to plead. The defence said he wasn't and claimed diminished responsibility, but you made hay of their psychiatrist and the prisoner got life, and a good thing, too. He was a public menace and had more than one murder to his credit, although he was only indicted for the death of an old lady. Shall I stick my neck out and suggest that, like me, you don't believe that girl's death was an accident?'

'I still have an open mind.'

'And that this idea of wanting to look at the cottage was only an excuse for having a look at *us*?'

'Dear me!' said Dame Beatrice admiringly.

'Well, now that's settled, I think we'll send my brother and Carleton off to the pub, while you and I settle down to have a good talk.'

'I should like that very much.' The younger men removed themselves and the host produced sherry.

'Well, now,' he said invitingly, 'let's pool our ideas.'

'I have very few to contribute. I was asked to make some enquiries, but, so far, little has resulted from them. I should be interested to know why you suspect foul play.'

'Well, like you, I don't exactly suspect it, but it seems to me a distinct possibility. I suppose the nature of my job conditions me. Our firm is sometimes concerned with cases of violent crime — muggings, rape, armed robbery, even murder – so I suppose I look on the violent or unexpected deaths of young women with a particularly jaundiced eye and, my word! — this specimen went about positively *begging* for trouble, as my young brother indicated.'

'I suppose – perhaps it is an unfair question – but I suppose you have no suspicions of anybody in particular?'

'No. She was quite promiscuous. One heard of skirmishes among the dunes and all that sort of thing. Chaps at the pub used to make jokes about her, you know. The better read called her Moll Flanders and to the coarser grained she was known as Eskimo Nell, so that will show you.'

'She was very young to have gained that sort of notoriety.'

'She gained it in so short a time, too. I have wondered whether somebody she knew at home – she was a Londoner, so the papers said – followed her down here with intent to do the deed, but it's only a theory.'

'What about the man who found the body?'

'Yes, I know. Interesting you should mention him. That's another matter on which I've pondered, but I guess the police investigated that possibility very thoroughly. After the deceased's nearest and dearest relatives, the person who finds the body becomes the number one suspect. The fellow is still down here, if you want to speak to him. He was out cockling early in the morning when he saw her lying there, or so he said at the inquest. I spoke to him afterwards.'

'*I* should like to speak to him. I doubt whether it is reasonable to suspect him, since I suppose that, if he was guilty, he would not have reported to the authorities. Simpler to have emulated the priest and the Levite, and passed by on the other side. There appear to have been no witnesses to his discovery of the body.'

'Well, none came forward, but it's quite extraordinary how many people do get up early on holiday so as to make the most of the day. Besides, there are the cockles to be had – they leave tell-tale marks on the sandy mudflats – and I believe you can also find small crabs. Some people – the locals mostly, I suspect – also gather edible samphire on the marshes. I don't think you could guarantee that *nobody* would spot you, however early in the morning it was, if you were up to a bit of no good, but nobody else came forward. Then there are the off-shore yachtsmen. They all carry binoculars and could have seen if anything fishy was going on.'

'I think the drowning – whether by accident or design – happened at night. In that case the cockler could quite innocently have come upon the body next morning. Will you give me his address?'

'I'll do better than that. I'll go with you to visit him, if you like.'

'That would be more than kind.'

The man's name was Sleach. He lodged with a widow who let rooms down by the Old Quay. This was now a jumble of cottages, most of them derelict. There were also some timber-built, black-tarred warehouses now in use only for storing fishermen's gear. A rotting duck-punt was pulled up on the stones and mud which formed part of the shore and a decrepit sailing barge, with its mast intact but its timbers beginning to rot away on the starboard side, was moored against the planks which formed a kind of continuous fender against the stonework of the cobbled quay.

' "Change and decay in all around I see",' murmured Dame Beatrice. Their quarry was not in.

'That do spend most of his evenings at the pub,' the landlady informed them.

'I'm a solicitor,' said Billington. 'Have you known him long?'

'He's my nephoo.'

'Oh, I see.'

'That's not in any money trouble?'

'No, no, nothing like that. It's in connection with that body he found on the beach.'

'I reckon that was a terrible sad thing an' all. Poor young mawther! But Billy only know what that testify at inquest. That don't hev further to say.'

'Surely not, but naturally the relatives are very much upset about the drowning and want as much information as they can get.'

The woman looked with some curiosity at Dame Beatrice.

'You'll be grandma, I whoolly think,' she said. Dame Beatrice inclined a gracious head.

'She was a wild girl, I'm afraid,' she observed, but the fish did not rise to this fly.

'I think,' said Billington, when they reached the pub, 'that I'd better go in and winkle him out. By the sound of it, the place is jam-packed. It's still early in the evening, so he won't be bottled yet and we may get something out of him which didn't get said at the inquest.'

The pub was on the New Quay. Here the houses and store places were well built of flint with fairly high-pitched roofs and the pub itself was a pleasant, much altered three-storey building with a low wall around its forecourt and some lath and plaster work around the windows.

Dame Beatrice strolled towards the sea wall. Some tidy little sailing-boats were lying out on the hard, a couple of rowing-boats without their oars lay near them, and a lifebelt hung on a wooden board near by. It was a strangely orderly scene after the decrepitude of the Old Quay and, except for the sociable hubbub from the pub which still came to her ears, exceptionally quiet and deserted.

Billington and his prey soon joined her, each with a pint tankard in his hand.

'Here's Mr Sleach, Dame Beatrice. There's a bench outside the pub. Shall we sit?' asked Billington, leading the way.

'Do you live in Saltacres, Mr Sleach?' Dame Beatrice asked, when they were seated.

'No. I work in Hull and take my summer fortnight with my auntie. I fare to go home tomorrow.'

'I am greatly concerned about the death of young Camilla

St John. Can you tell me exactly how you came to find her body? I did not know of the inquest until it was too late for me to attend it.'

'This gentleman tell me he's a lawyer. No trouble in it for me, is there?'

'Oh, no. He is merely escorting me and will know all the helpful questions to ask, that's all.'

'What I hev to say I said at the inquest.'

'Yes, I know, but I wasn't there to hear it. Please begin at the beginning and tell me all you can.'

'Oh, well, then, I go out early to get the cockles. They make a nice start to a meal with thin bread and butter. The visitors they go for to uncover them with their bare hands, but, being local born, though now I live in Hull, I know a better trick than that, so I take my cockling knife, give one little turn and up come the cockle.'

'Ah, yes, the expert at work.'

'Well, I obtain a nice little foo – coupla dozen or more – then I straighten up and shake the cockles – real Creeky Blues – down in my bucket to make more room. Then I spot something lying half in the water and half out. Tide was on the turn, so I say to myself that the last tide brought something in, so I go over and take a look and I find this poor young girl.'

'So what did you do then?'

'I go on with my cockling as soon as I know there's nawthen I can do for her. Then when I reckon I get enough for auntie and me with our tea, I go back and tell auntie what I see. Her say to go to pub and 'phone police, so I do that and that's the lot.'

'When you had finished your cockling, was the body exactly as you had seen it first?'

'Well, as to that, how could it be? Tide was on the turn, so I pull the poor thing up above highwater mark soon as I see what it was.'

'Did you turn your back on it while you went on gathering your cockles?'

'Times, yes, and times, no. You hev to take the cockles where they fare to be. That don't grow in rows like turnips or sugar beet.'

'Did you see any living person on the beach or the dunes?'

'A fair way off there were other folk getting the cockles.'

'But they did not come near you or the corpse?'

'When they go, they go the other way, towards the church.'

'Was the corpse clothed?'

'She hev a kind of little bodice that hardly cover her breasts (not that she hev much up there to cover) and a little pair of bathing drawers that hardly cover — '

'Yes, a bikini. I see. What about the clothes she must have taken off before she bathed?'

'Oo, I wouldn' know nawthen about any other garments but those I describe. Now I come to recollect, though, Crowner did ask the gentleman who spoke to knowing the body — '

'Mr Kirby?'

'That's him.'

'The coroner asked Mr Kirby about the girl's clothes?'

'Yes, that did. The gentleman said the young woman was liable to run straight out of the cottage in her bathers and, when she'd had her dip, that would lie out on the doons and dry off.'

'What about shoes?'

'I couldn't go for to say.'

'Well, she might have done all that in the sunshine, although I think she would have worn shoes of some sort to cross the marshes,' said Billington, 'but at night she surely would have something on over her bikini and have taken a towel with her? It gets chilly at night when there's no sun to dry you.'

'I couldn't speak as to any of that, but if she had any clo'es and a pair of shoes, I reckon she left 'em on the doons out of tide reach and the Old Mole had 'em.'

'And who is the Old Mole?' Dame Beatrice enquired.

'That's an old mumper live by himself and talk foreign. When he ent mumpin', that scavenge up and down the place looking for driftwood or empty bottles, or maybe bits of sandwiches and cake left behind by picnickers, or anything else that's there. Proper old jackdaw. Pick up whatever take his fancy.'

'Oh, a beachcomber,' said Billington. 'And where is he to be found?'

'That doss down in a shed on the Old Quay.'

'Oh, a neighbour of yours!'

'That's harmless. We pass the time of day.'

'What, exactly, is a mumper?' Dame Beatrice enquired. 'The word is new to me.'

'Dialect for beggar,' Billington explained. 'Why is he called the Old Mole?' he asked Sleach.

'On account that purtend to be blind. Carry a white stick, but that's only to poke about with. Help him in his mumpin' to let the visitors think he's blind. Makes them feel sorry for him, if you take my meaning, but that's an old fraud, that is. Can see as well as you and me, and don't miss nawthen if there's anything worth picking up on the beach or among the doons.'

'He sounds an interesting and enterprising character. So you think, Mr Sleach, that if the dead girl's clothes had been left on the shore, this man will have found and kept them? Maybe he has sold them by now.'

'Too fly for that, I reckon, ma'am. That wait until all the fuss die down. If he hev the poor young mawther's clo'es, they're still in his shack.'

'Then I must ask him to produce them.'

'We'll come with you,' said Billington.

'No. My thanks for the chivalrous thought, but that will be quite unnecessary. I see that my man has followed me up with the car. He will escort me and I have no doubt, Mr Sleach, that your aunt will be good enough to point out where this man lives. I am most grateful for your assistance, both of you.'

'A pleasure,' said Billington. 'Come on, then, Sleach. I can do with another pint and so can you.' He walked over to the car with Dame Beatrice and added, 'I can see you don't want to involve Sleach any further. Will you let me know how you get on with the Old Mole?'

'It is the least I can do, although I expect nothing to come of my visit to him.'

'Would it help your enquiry if it does turn out that he picked up the girl's clothes?'

'To a certain extent, I think it would, particularly if he is willing to tell me which day he found them. She does not appear to have returned to her cottage on the night of the moonlight bathe she took with a friend, so the inference is that

that is the night on which she was drowned, but, so far, that has not been proved.'

'Ah, yes, the medical evidence was more than a bit sketchy regarding the actual time of death, I remember. But if the Old Mole does have the clothes, isn't that going to be a bit awkward for the – for her fellow bather?'

'He is already under some supicion.'

She got into the car and gave George directions to take her back to the Old Quay.

CHAPTER 11

THE OLD MOLE

'Those who go beneath the surface do so at their peril.'
Oscar Wilde

Digging out the Old Mole proved to be a matter of no difficulty. Dame Beatrice reintroduced herself to Sleach's aunt. The beggarman's domicile, the least disreputable of the rotting warehouses, was pointed out with the warning that it was probably infested with rats, undoubtedly stank and, in any case, was no place for a lady.

Dame Beatrice enquired whether the old man had ever engaged the interest of the police, and was reassured.

'That's harmless. Fossick about on the shore, after the tide go out, for bits of wood, and room the doons for bottles and old tins. Like a jackdaw, that is, for anything that shine. What he do with the things nobody know for certain, but, with a bit of mumping, that live.'

Without being asked, but with a set, masculine expression on his face, George accompanied his employer to the building which had been pointed out. He was carrying a heavy spanner wrapped in a piece of brown paper to conceal its real nature and appearance. His alternative means of persuasion was in the form of a couple of tall cans of beer which he carried in the long pockets of the overalls he had assumed when Dame Beatrice had indicated the scope of their enterprise.

Knowing him, she deduced the nature of his precautions and observing merely that the carrot often produced better results than the bludgeon, and that she anticipated 'none of what Mrs. Gavin would call the rough stuff, George,' she kicked with a firmly shod foot at the rickety door. It flew open and disclosed the interior of the warehouse.

The bursting in of the door had caused the two sets of

shutters, one on the north, the other on the east side, to fly open as well, so there was sufficient light to disclose the contents of the big shack. These included an elderly man wearing frayed trousers and what had been an Army greatcoat over a sweater. He came forward leaning on a crook-handled, white-painted stick.

He was unkempt, but not filthy, and although the building gave forth an odour of closeness and human occupation, to say that it stank would have been an exaggeration, Dame Beatrice thought. He said,

'If it be you boys, go away. You know I can't see you, so stop tormenting of me.'

'Mr Mole, I presume,' said Dame Beatrice.

'That's a lady's voice. I don't want no soup kitchens. I manage all right on my own. Salvation Army, is it?'

'You know very well that it is not. Where are my granddaughter's clothes?'

The old man put what to him was a pertinent query.

'I ent in trouble with police?'

'Answer my question, please.'

'You ent no right.'

'I have every right.'

'Come clean. It will be the better for you,' said George, in a deep, histrionic growl.

'I don't know nothing about no clothes.'

'Think again,' Dame Beatrice advised him. 'My granddaughter went swimming and left her things on the beach. I have reason to think you found them. Will you hand them over, or do you want the police to come for them?'

'Make your mind up, chummie,' said George, to the great admiration of his employer. 'Stealing by finding is an offence under the law.'

'I ent stole nothing. What's left on beach is mine.'

'That may be true of flotsam and jetsam,' said Dame Beatrice. 'It is *not* true of property left on the beach by persons who have every intention of returning to claim it.'

'What if they'm buried it, then? What about that? That's buried treasure, that's what that is.'

'Buried it?'

'Ah, that's right. They buried it in the sand.'

'In the dunes?'

'That's right. So I digs her up, see, and now she's mine.'

'Oh, no, she isn't, not if she belonged to madam's relative,' said George. 'I reckon, if she buried it, it was to hide it away from people like you. So come on, matie. Hand over.'

'I don't want trouble.'

'Of course you don't, so stop being an Artful Dodger,' said Dame Beatrice.

'And keep your nose clean,' said George, 'or my superiors will be taking an interest in your doings.'

'I reckon to sell what I find.'

'Yes, but not what you steal,' said Dame Beatrice. 'You are not a native of these parts, I think.' She now realised what, to Sleach, 'talk foreign' meant.

'Why you figure that out?' the beachcomber enquired.

'Because the local people are honest.'

'Will you gimme something for my trouble? I been taking good care of that there bit of luggage till I find out who it belong to.'

'Produce it,' said Dame Beatrice, scarcely believing that she had heard him pronounce the word *luggage,* 'and then we will talk of rewards.'

'All right, then. I don't want no trouble.' He limped to the back of the shack where there was an opening which, judging from the configuration of the building seen from outside, led, Dame Beatrice thought, to a much more extensive part of the old warehouse. He emerged carrying a suitcase. 'Buried, her was,' he said, in a beggar's whine. 'How were I to know as somebody wanted her back?' He dumped it down in front of them and waited. Dame Beatrice fished out a pound note and gave it to him. George disembarrassed himself of the cans of beer and put them down in the doorway before he picked up the suitcase and followed Dame Beatrice to what remained of the sea wall of the quay.

'An outrageous and unkind bluff, George,' she said, as he set the suitcase on the coping. 'It is a dreadful thing to take advantage of the old and indigent.'

'Take advantage nothing, madam,' said George sturdily as Dame Beatrice opened the suitcase. 'He would never have got a pound for flogging any stuff that's in here, and the case itself is only one of those cardboard type things, and battered about, at that.'

'Mr Kirby, in his letter, said that the girl would have been wearing jeans and a sweater. I notice the jeans, but the sweater appears to be missing.'

'I fancy that old scoundrel was wearing it, madam.'

'That would explain its absence from the suitcase, except that I do not believe it was put into the suitcase until after the girl's death. Well, loth as I am to inform on the Old Mole, the police will have to be told. They are still looking for the suitcase.'

'If I may ask, madam, how did you know this man had it?'

'I did not know he had it. From what we were told by Mr Sleach, I guessed he might have collected the drowned girl's outer garments which she would have shed before she entered the water, but finding the suitcase went far beyond my expectations, and the place in which it was found goes a long way towards proving Mr Kirby's conviction that the girl was murdered. No girl in her senses would carry a suitcase across the marshes for the pleasure of carrying it back again when she had had her bathe.'

'Not even if she did not intend to return to her friends, madam?'

'I think not. There are plenty of places near the road where she could have hidden it, not to speak of the boot of a car. If she had intended to leave the Kirbys, she would not have gone off alone. From what I have been told about her, a man would have been involved.'

'He might have been her murderer, don't you think, madam?'

'I think that whoever took that suitcase down to the sand-dunes and buried it so shallowly was pressed for time and is almost certainly the murderer. I also believe that the girl herself had no idea that the suitcase had ever left the cottage.'

The county police were sceptical, but not completely unimpressed.

'We'll look into it, Dame Beatrice, of course,' said the Inspector. 'The man who found the suitcase ought to have turned it in, and he must have known he ought. We've got that much to go on.'

'I trust no charges will be pressed. I have committed myself, I fear, to a promise that there will be no repercussions.'

'Mr Kirby or his wife will have to identify the suitcase and its contents, but so far as the finder is concerned, I daresay a warning that findings are not keepings will be sufficient to impress him. We know all about him and he's never been in trouble. You say he gave up the suitcase without any bother?'

'Oh, yes. I think it might be interesting to find out exactly where it was buried.'

'And, if it *was* buried, how he came upon it – unless, of course, he knew exactly where to look.'

'You mean he may have witnessed its interment? Most unlikely, I would have thought. More probably, the strong winds blew the loose sand away and uncovered it.'

'We'll find out, I dare say. Anyway, thank you for your information, Dame Beatrice. I'll have a little talk with the chap and get the suitcase identified, and then we'll see, but, unless he murdered the girl and then pinched the suitcase, I don't think the verdict at the inquest will be easily upset.'

'You really think that a girl intent upon a moonlight bathe would have carried all her belongings across the marshes?'

'You never know what ideas girls get in their heads, madam, especially runaways.'

'You do realise, Inspector, don't you? – that, except for this very dubious business of the suitcase, there is no evidence that the poor child ever intended to leave her friends at all.'

'That, Dame Beatrice, amounts to the serious implication that if Miss Hoveton St John didn't remove the suitcase from the holiday cottage, one of its other inmates did. Can you substantiate that?'

'My statement does not necessarily implicate the other tenants, but I admit it does seem rather far-fetched to suppose that anybody else entered the cottage, packed the suitcase, enticed the girl into the sea and drowned her.'

'So you *do* think one of her friends did it!'

'Unless the verdict at the inquest was the correct one, I hardly know what else to think.'

'The verdict at the inquest mostly likely *was* the correct one, but we shall keep an eye on things and if you get hold of any more evidence, I'm sure you'll let us know. Meanwhile, we'll put the breeze up that mumping old vagabond and also put out a few feelers elsewhere. We know your reputation, madam, and a hint from you is worth thinking over. Did any of them stand to gain anything by the girl's death, I wonder? A pity they're not still here, but there! When there's trouble round here it's the visitors who cause it. We shall have to get some co-operation from the London end. I took Mr Kirby's London address when I spoke to him before the inquest and I daresay he knows where the rest of his party can be found. They are all Londoners, I believe.'

Dame Beatrice had had her interview at the police station in Stack Ferry on the day following the discovery of the suitcase. Back at The Stadholder she decided to pay another visit to the Hamiltons on the following day. Mrs Hamilton herself answered the door and invited her in.

'I must not stay. I am on my way to lunch,' said Dame Beatrice, 'but there is a question I would like to ask you, if I may.'

'Do come in and ask it. I am quite alone in the house. It's the maid's day off, and my husband and son have gone out in the yacht. You'll take a glass of sherry?'

'If you are alone, why don't we both lunch at my hotel? My car is outside and my man can bring you back at any time which suits you.'

'That would be very nice. I'll just go up and change and leave a note for my husband in case they get back early. What is your question?'

'You may think it a strange one, but I have a good reason for asking it. As woman to woman, what did you think of that young Camilla Hoveton St John?'

'I have a superstition about speaking ill of the dead.'

'I feel you have answered me.'

'Well, to tell you the truth, Dame Beatrice, I thought she was quite appalling, and I was annoyed and rather worried when my son brought her on board. Fortunately, when we rounded the Point on the return trip, the sea became rather boisterous.'

'Fortunately?'

'Yes. We are all good sailors, but the girl was violently sick.

Nothing puts a young man off so completely as seeing the admired object in the throes of extreme nausea. The poor girl was quite revolting and I'm ashamed to say that I was glad of it. I did not want my son to continue the acquaintanceship. It was quite unsuitable in every way. He is still at university and very impressionable.'

'I understand that for a short time they bathed together. Did he comment at all on her prowess as a swimmer?'

'Yes, he was quite impressed by it.'

'Did he make any comment when it was known that she had drowned?'

'He said he could hardly believe it. The girl had told him about a friend of hers, a man, a very powerful swimmer, who had been foolish enough to bathe off Saltacres on an outgoing tide and had experienced great difficulty in getting back to safety. My son said that unless the girl had intended suicide, he did not believe she would ever have taken such a risk. *Could* it have been suicide, Dame Beatrice?'

'It is possible, of course. Did you form any opinion as to her state of mind while she was with you?'

'Her state of mind (except that she was making open overtures to my son) did not concern me. She seemed perfectly happy, so far as I could tell, although, obviously, the presence of my husband and myself rather cramped her style. When we reached the bird sanctuary, which was our objective, she soon detached my son from us, and they wandered off, as you know, to bathe.'

'Did your son ever show any sign of intending to meet Miss St John again?' asked Dame Beatrice, when they were in the car.

Mrs Hamilton laughed.

'I think the bout of sea-sickness would have given romance a mortal blow,' she said. 'At any rate, he never did meet her again unless he slipped out after we had gone to bed, but, if he had done that, I should have heard the sound of the car. I am a very indifferent sleeper. He would hardly have *walked* over to Saltacres, where she informed us she had a holiday cottage. It is over thirty miles from here.'

'Your yacht?'

'At night? And without his father to help him? Impossible, I would think. Rounding the Point is a tricky operation, and my son is still a novice at sailing.' She paused and then said: 'I am not sure I like your questions very much, Dame Beatrice. Is there something behind them?'

'I appreciate your feelings. The questions are only to clear the air. You see, Mrs Hamilton, I have been briefed to enquire into what I am now quite convinced was a case not of accident or suicide, but of murder.'

'So my son has indicated, and I refuse to be associated with anything so dreadful.'

'I was obliged to ask the questions. You have answered them.'

'All the same — '

'Please do not distress yourself. I have met your son, remember. All I have done is to clear him out of the way. To tell you the truth, this is just as likely – I am beginning to think *more* likely – to have been a jealous woman's crime. It need not concern a man.'

'In that case, you might as well suspect *me* as suspect my son!'

'Oh, I do, and to exactly the same extent,' said Dame Beatrice, with her crocodile grin. 'I do not suspect either of you of having had more than a few hours' completely innocent acquaintance with Miss St John.'

'But, Dame Beatrice, you will have to tell me more than that!'

'Yes, of course I shall. Miss St John's luggage disappeared from the cottage at which she was staying, and the police have been looking for it. It was found by a beachcomber. He was searching the beach and the sand-dunes at Saltacres, as was his custom, when he came upon the suitcase partly buried in the sand. He impounded it, that is all.'

'But what was it doing there?'

'My theory, which, I may add, the police do not wholly accept, is that the murderer hoped to hide it in order to give the impression that the girl herself had taken it out of the cottage and was not intending to return. I think he may have hoped, also, that if the body turned up again, it would have been in the sea and among the sea-creatures so long that it would be unrecognisable.'

'That sounds to me like someone who had no knowledge of

how the tides run in these parts. Such a person is unlikely to have been a yachtsman, so my family is in the clear, I suppose, simply because of that.'

'Mrs Hamilton, you must not allow me to offend you. The discovery of the girl's suitcase in the place where it was found convinces me that I am investigating a case of murder. Any help which I can get from anybody who met Camilla St John may turn out to be the pivot on which the whole case turns.'

'My son tells me that you do a lot of this kind of work.'

'Sometimes it fits in with my commitments to the Home Office; sometimes, as in this instance, it is simply because of a desire to find out the truth. One more question?'

'I suppose so.'

'Are you certain you saw the girl meet and go off with a man in a car?'

'Oh, yes, I am perfectly certain. When we moored after our trip to the bird sanctuary we landed the girl and then I remembered that I had to call for some food I had ordered from the Chinese take-away shop. I had the girl in my sights — she did not look round and, in any case, I had neither the wish nor the intention to follow her. There was a short cut through the public car park. I took it and saw her get into a car in which a man was already sitting.'

'Can you describe him?'

'Except that he was bearded, no.'

A bearded man might as well be Adrian Kirby as anybody else, Dame Beatrice thought. In any case, Camilla had arrived safely back in Saltacres that night. There seemed nothing more to be gained by enquiries at Stack Ferry or from the Hamiltons.

CHAPTER 12

PALGRAVE AGAIN

' "Right, as usual," said the Duchess. "What a clear way you have of putting things!" '

Lewis Carroll

Apart from impounding the suitcase and testing it for fingerprints, the police took no action except to point out to the Old Mole that finders were not always entitled to be keepers. They checked the fingerprints against those of the old beachcomber and found, most unsurprisingly, that they tallied. There were other prints, legible enough, but not able to be checked because they were not on record and as Adrian, Miranda, Palgrave and any number of unknown people could have handled the suitcase quite legitimately, there was nothing to be gained from the prints.

Dame Beatrice saw the Inspector again before she left Stack Ferry, but visited no other of the acquaintances she and George had made either there or at Saltacres. The Lowsons, she knew, had concluded their holiday before Dame Beatrice left her hotel for her home and then London. What she felt might be a crucial interview was yet to come, and it was not with them.

She returned to the Stone House in Hampshire, dealt again with correspondence and then put through a telephone call to Adrian's flat. He gave her Palgrave's number.

'I wanted to keep in touch with him,' he said. 'Have you made any progress, I wonder, with you know what?'

'Very little. I am being forced to conclude that we may have to accept the verdict.'

'But you yourself? What do you think?'

'The same as you do, but the evidence is not there. When I have visited Mr Palgrave I will come and talk to you and see whether you have any suggestions to offer.'

Palgrave, she realised, was likely to be still on school holiday and might not be at home, but she rang his number hopefully and found that he was in. He was not best pleased at being disturbed.

'Who *are* you?' he asked. 'I'm terribly busy.'

'I am the Home Office psychiatrist. My name is Bradley.'

'Oh, yes? Are you one of the bees in Adrian Kirby's bonnet?'

'I am the queen bee, Mr Palgrave. Will you see me?'

'I suppose so, but I'm up to my eyes in work. I'm writing a book. Can you manage half past two any day this week? I generally take a short break after lunch, so that's my best time.'

'Half past two on Wednesday, then. Thank you so much. Goodbye.'

'Uncouth cub!' said Ferdinand, who was visiting his mother again and who, at her suggestion, had been listening on the extension.

'No, no. I expect he *is* very busy if he is writing a book,' she said. 'I shall not keep him long. All I want from him is an exact account of how he spent the evening on which the girl appears to have left the cottage for good, either with or without her suitcase.'

Palgrave, who, in spite of the tone he had employed over the telephone, appeared to be well-mannered, greeted her courteously.

'Adrian told me you were looking into this rotten affair,' he said, 'but I think you're wasting your time. Camilla did a damn' silly thing and got drowned. There's nothing else to be found out.'

'So I am beginning to believe – not that there is nothing else to find out, but that my enquiry has foundered.'

'Well, bad luck, of course, but I hope Adrian will be satisfied. You don't really believe it was murder, do you?'

'I am hoping that you will be able to persuade me that it was not.'

'How do I go about persuading you?'

'Well, except for the murderer – if there was one – you appear to have been the last person to have seen the girl alive. I understand that you returned to the cottage that night— '

'Only to change my clothes and pick up my things!'

'Quite – leaving Miss St John in the sea.'

'Swimming about as merrily as a young water-beetle, I assure you. The tide certainly hadn't turned when I left her.'

'Of course not. I suppose one of the "things" you picked up at the cottage was not Miss St John's suitcase?'

'Good Lord, no! – only my own.'

'You had not already put that in the boot of your car? – before you took the others for an evening drink, I mean.'

'No, I hadn't. I only intended to *sleep* in the car. I was going back to the cottage for breakfast. I thought I could collect my traps then.'

'But you abandoned that plan. Why, Mr Palgrave?'

Palgrave faced her with hostile, suspicious eyes.

'Look, what *is* this?' he said angrily; but it was the anger of fear, she surmised. 'You don't think *I* had anything to do with that wretched kid's death, do you?'

'I am waiting for you to convince me that you had not. Her suitcase has been found, you know.'

'Well, if she took it out of the cottage, it was bound to turn up sooner or later, I suppose.'

'It turned up in an unexpected place and under what I consider were very suspicious circumstances.'

'Oh? How do you mean?'

'Never mind. I may tell you later. First I must hear your own account of that evening and why you changed your plans about breakfasting at the cottage.'

'Oh, that's easily explained. Look here – ' he had abandoned his belligerent attitude and spoke quietly, almost placatingly – 'please tell me what all this is about, won't you? Am I being accused of anything?'

'I am not in a position to accuse anybody. Tell me your story of that night and the following morning.'

'I suppose,' said Palgrave, half ruefully, half humorously, 'you can check what I tell you about myself?'

'To a certain extent, yes, unless Mrs Kirby and Mr Lowson have been lying to me.'

'What did they say?'

'I will fill in the gaps if you leave any.'

'You're a hard nut to crack, Dame Beatrice. Does anybody know you are here?'

'Oh, yes, my son knows, and so does Mr Kirby. I always make certain that more than one person knows where I am when I am employed on Home Office business.'

'I thought Adrian Kirby was employing you.'

'I do not accept employment from private persons in cases where there is a suspicion that murder has been committed. Mr Kirby drew my attention to this case, that is all. I could hardly invoke the assistance of the police if— '

'Oh, the police are still in on this, are they? I was under the impression that they had accepted the verdict given at the inquest, and were going to leave me alone.'

'The discovery of the suitcase— '

'Oh, that damned suitcase!'

' — may have shaken their complacency a little, I fancy. So now, since you are a busy man, let us have your account and then I can be gone and leave you to your writing. How is the book going?'

Palgrave smiled for the first time during the interview.

'Marvellously!' he said. 'Of course I'm finding one or two snags. I suppose every writer does. Apart from that, the thing almost writes itself. I spent months trying to get the right idea, but when it came there was no holding it. Of course I'm only on the first draft and I can see already how I can polish up certain bits, but the main theme is dead right. I know that in my bones. It's all I can do not to show it around to my friends and have them tell me how damned good it is, but most people shy away from reading a typescript and say they'll wait until they can get the book from the library.'

'I am delighted to hear that you are making such good progress with it. You are still on holiday?'

'Yes. I shall have to slow up when I begin school again, but I shall have the book so well set by then that it won't matter all that much. Those marshes have been sheer inspiration.'

' "Mud, mud, glorious mud, Nothing quite like it for cooling the blood" ', carolled Dame Beatrice, to her hearer's astonishment.

'Yes, well, you wanted to hear how I spent that evening,' he said. 'Where do you want me to begin?'

'Did you dislike Miss St John?'

'What a question to ask me when you think somebody murdered her!'

'Well, did you dislike her? And why did you leave the cottage?'

'Dislike her, no. She wouldn't have been a bad little bint if only she'd had a bit more sense, but I got sick to death of it when she insisted on pursuing me when I was trying to work out something for my novel. I could have wrung her skinny little neck! All the same, I didn't drown her.'

'Plainly and clearly stated.'

'It's perfectly true, I assure you. I decided to leave the cottage when I discovered my former fiancée and her husband there. The Kirbys were a bit upset when I said I was leaving, but the situation was too much for me to cope with. All the same, I didn't just want to walk out on the Kirbys. They had been very kind to me, and Morag didn't seem to bear me any grudge. Although I'd jilted her she seemed friendly, so I suggested a little farewell party at the pub, all drinks on me.'

'So where was Miss St John? Did she know what you had planned?'

'I don't think we'd seen Camilla all day. Oh, wait a minute, though. I didn't see her myself, but I think the others must have done. She was at supper with us the night before, I'm certain, and she must have been there at the next breakfast with the others – this was before Morag and Lowson turned up, of course – but I didn't see her then because I got my own breakfast that morning and had it early and went over to Stack Ferry for the day, and Camilla wasn't there when I got back in the evening.'

'And this was *before* Mr and Mrs Lowson arrived at the cottage? You are sure of that?'

'Oh, yes. I had the shock of my life when I got back in the evening and found them there.'

'And Miss St John was not there when you got back? – so you really did not see her all that day? Are you *sure*?'

'Yes. Otherwise I would have invited her to go with us to the pub. I didn't grudge the little limpet a couple of drinks. Of course I did see her later when we had our moonlight dip.'

'If you did not see her all day, perhaps she had given up

pursuing you.'

'As to that, I'd had a bit of a toss-up with her because the day before (I think it was) she had sneaked off with Adrian in my car, of all the damn' cheek, and I'd rather told her what I thought of her.'

'And when your little party at the public house was over?'

'Ah, we're coming to the point now, I suppose you think.'

'Well, I think that what you are about to tell me may prove interesting, if not particularly useful.'

'You won't be able to check it, but I'll tell you the truth.'

Dame Beatrice waited. It seemed that Palgrave was assembling his thoughts, or perhaps his memories, and arranging them in some sort of order. At last she asked:

'Is the truth so complicated?'

'Eh? Oh, sorry! I was just thinking. Well, when we left the pub I got into my car to spend the night on the back seat, as I thought, but it was so chilly and downright uncomfortable that I soon had to get out and tramp up and down for a bit to warm up and get the stiffness out of my legs. It was bright moonlight and that's how I came to spot Camilla coming towards the car.'

'From which direction?'

'Oh, from the cottage, of course.'

'Carrying her suitcase?'

'No, she wasn't carrying anything like that, so far as I remember; she certainly wasn't carrying a suitcase. She had a towel, I think.'

'So you met and she suggested a moonlight bathe.'

'That's it. My swim-trunks were back at the cottage in my suitcase, of course, but I didn't think they mattered at night with nobody about. It seemed a long way across the marshes to the sea, but Camilla held my hand and sang all sorts of rather maudlin little songs, some in French – *Si j'étais l'oiseau des bois* – that sort of thing – and some in English – '

'What was she wearing?'

'Wearing? Oh, her usual gear of jeans and a sweater. She was wearing her bikini underneath.'

'And you?'

'Grey flannels, shirt and blazer. I'd packed my sweaters. I could have done with a sweater in the car, but walking was all right and I made sure we kept up a solid tramping. There's a causeway that crosses a little bridge and takes you as far as the dunes, so I took her along at pretty well marching pace. All I wanted was to walk and swim, not to indulge in a bit of dalliance among the marsh-plants.'

'You preferred that it should operate among the sand-dunes, no doubt.'

Palgrave laughed.

'Not I,' he said. 'There was a very nasty, penetrating night wind blowing. We stripped off and I went straight into deep water.'

'*Deep* water?'

'Yes, the tide must have been almost full. Anyway, it was still coming in. Almost at once the water was waist-high and in no time at all it was deep enough for swimming. I didn't stay in long. I followed my usual practice of going out until I couldn't touch the bottom when I put my feet down, and then swimming level with the shore for a hundred metres or so, then turning and swimming back. I think I only did this a couple of times before I got out.'

'But Miss St John remained in the water?'

'Well, no, not exactly. She called out to know what I was doing and when I called back that I was getting dressed she called me by a rude name which I won't repeat, and joined me on shore.'

'Ah, yes.'

'Oh, *no!* I told her if she wanted to play games among the sand-dunes to choose a nice sunny day. I said I was wet and was getting cold and all I wanted was to dry myself, get some clothes on and walk briskly back to my car. She said I was no sort of sport, but I threatened what I'd do if she didn't either dress or get back in the sea.'

'Most praiseworthy!'

'There is no need to jibe. I simply didn't want any of that sort of thing. There had been just one occasion on a lovely day when we had bathed together and were lying out on the sand-dunes and the sand was soft and warm and there were seagulls white and lovely against the blue of the sky and I was feeling relaxed and the girl was naked – well, that was one thing – but at night, with a chilly wind and my wet body that only asked to be warm and dry and clothed, there was no temptation at all. In fact, the little devil's attempts to blackmail me only nauseated me because I'd seen and spoken to Morag that day and evening. My mind was full of *her*. I wanted her pretty badly and I knew I couldn't have her. I'd chucked my chances away and I felt savage with Camilla, who was offering herself as a substitute. I could have murdered her – but I didn't. I dried myself on my shirt and went back to the cottage.'

'Leaving Miss St John to go back into the sea? Did you actually see her do this?'

'Oh, yes. When she found there was nothing doing, I think the cold wind drove her back into the water. It was definitely warmer in the sea than on land.'

'Did you have the beach and the dunes entirely to yourselves?'

'The beach, yes. The dunes I can't answer for. They are all dips, rises and hollows, as perhaps you know, and a lot of holidaymaking youngsters sleep rough. I wouldn't be surprised if there were couples snugged down here and there. I wasn't aware of anybody, but that says nothing. Even by daylight you can pretty nearly tread on them if you're not careful.'

'You saw nobody walking across the marshes?'

'Not a soul while I was on them. There was a bit of white mist I half thought was somebody, but it wasn't.'

'Well, now, so far, Mr Palgrave, your story lacks corroboration, but, from the time you reached the cottage that night until the time you left it, I have been given one or two pieces of information about your movements.'

'So I'd better watch my step? Fair enough. Well, I got back to the cottage—'

'Why not to your car?'

'I knew I'd never get to sleep in it, so I opted to sneak into the cottage and get my things and then take the car out Stack Ferry way and drive around until breakfast time.'

'And at the cottage—?'

'Ah, yes. That's where you've got the drop on me, isn't it? I went in as quietly as I could, because, of course, the front door opened straight into the room which had been mine before the Lowsons took it over, and I didn't want to wake them if they had gone to sleep. Then I crept about trying to locate my suitcase. There was nowhere in the room to hang up clothes or stick things in drawers, so I'd been living in and out of the suitcase for days, but they had moved it and I had to grope around for it, not liking to put on the light.

'I decided to change my clothes before appearing at the hotel in Stack Ferry – I was hoping, you see, that they could have me a day or two early, although my booking didn't actually start until the weekend – but then it occurred to me that if I changed in the parlour I might wake the Lowsons up, so, knowing that Camilla's room would be empty until she came back from her bathe, I sneaked upstairs with my suitcase and changed up there.

'I wasn't going to bother about shaving. I thought there would certainly be a barber's shop somewhere in Stack Ferry where I could get a shave and a trim before I went to the hotel, but I altered my mind.'

'Did you see Miss St John's suitcase when you used her room?'

'Not that I remember, but I wasn't noticing much. I wanted to be quick in case Camilla came back and found me in possession.'

'Did you see her night attire anywhere in the room?'

'I don't suppose she had any, you know. Child of nature and all that. Of course I suppose she could have tidied it away – stuck it in a drawer or under the pillow or something – but, judging from the state of the room, I shouldn't think it very likely.'

'So, having completed your preparations for departure, you left the cottage.'

'That's right, after I'd shaved in the kitchen. There wasn't a bathroom.'

'*With your own suitcase* you left the cottage?'

'Quite — and not with Camilla's, as the police seemed to think.'

'You have referred to the Lowsons. Can you be sure that the *Kirbys* were in the cottage while you were changing your clothes in Miss St John's room?'

'Be sure? Well, Mrs Kirby saw me leave the cottage after I'd shaved. She was at the bedroom window.'

'So she said.'

'Don't you believe her?'

'I believe nothing without proof. You see, it might be just as well for the Kirbys to appear to produce some evidence that they were in the cottage at that particular time.'

'Good heavens! You don't suppose Miranda Kirby drowned Camilla, do you? She can't even swim.'

'How do you know that?'

'She said she couldn't. Adrian couldn't, either. They never bathed in the sea.'

'She *said* she couldn't? You are singularly trusting, Mr Palgrave. What did Mrs Kirby think about Miss St John?'

'Just that she was a thundering little nuisance, that's all.'

'You said that you had a difference of opinion with Miss St John when she borrowed your car without permission and went to Stack Ferry in it.'

'She fully deserved the ticking-off I gave her.'

'She took Mr Kirby with her on this jaunt?'

'She took good care to lose him as soon as they got to Stack Ferry, I expect. I bet she only took him with her so that I shouldn't blow my top about the car. She was mistaken. I did blow my top. Of course, if Adrian had known she had snitched the car without permission, he would never have gone with her. I'm certain of that. Adrian is a very decent chap, one of the best. He can be a bit tedious at times – you know – tiresomely informative and all that, but — '

'We wander from the point, Mr Palgrave.'

'Which is, I take it, that I can't prove I did not drown Camilla before I went back that night and changed my clothes. One person I can definitely swear was in the cottage at the same time as I was, because I actually saw him asleep in the parlour, and that's Lowson.'

'Ah, yes. You left Miss St John in the sea — '

'Yes, and swimming about like a little fish.'

'I was not suggesting anything else. You returned to the cottage. How did you say you got in?'

'I had a key, but when I had changed and shaved and gone out again, I remember that I did not close the door behind me for fear of waking Lowson.'

'So you did not wake him when you entered the cottage?'

'Apparently not. Surprising, in a way, because I had to hunt around for my suitcase. They'd moved it from where I'd left it. I think I told you that. I had to find it before I could change my clothes, of course.'

'How long did all this take you?'

'Half an hour or so. Yes, quite that.'

'And Miss St John did not return?'

'Not while I was there.'

'And Mrs Lowson?'

'Oh, I see! Now that I remember, she wasn't there. I expect she was out enjoying the moonlight. She used to say it made her fey. Highland blood, you know.'

'Miss St John's suitcase was found half buried in a sand-dune, and I cannot believe that she herself took it there and hid it.'

'That does seem a bit odd, unless she had hidden it there earlier, before we bathed. She would have had plenty of time while we were all at the pub that evening.'

'Not a new suggestion, but why should she do such a thing?'

'Well, if she'd decided to flit when she knew the Lowsons were going to stay, and she had no place to leave a suitcase, I suppose she *might* have carried it down to the dunes, although it doesn't seem very likely unless she was expecting somebody to pick her up in a dinghy, but, even so, hardly at night.'

'I wonder whether Miss St John had a similar reason to your own for vacating the cottage?'

'How do you mean, Dame Beatrice?'

'That she had known the Lowsons – or one of them – before, and did not welcome them as house-mates.'

'I think she was simply planning to go on a toot with some bloke. Ever so much more likely, in my opinion, and I knew her, whereas you did not.'

'How right you are!'

'But the suitcase remains a mystery.'

'The person who buried it (and so inadequately!) remains a mystery.'

'Is it just because of the suitcase that you talk about a murderer?'

'Oh, dear me, no! Do *you* think Miss St John would have bathed in deep water on an outgoing tide?'

'No, I don't. What's more, on that particular evening the tide was pretty high, as I said, but it wasn't nearly on the turn when I left her. It could have had as much as an hour to run before there was slack water and then the ebb. Even Camilla wouldn't have stayed in as long as that.'

'The murderer can hardly have been a local person. He or she thought, no doubt, that the ebb would carry the body right out to sea, not knowing that, at Saltacres, what the sea removes it returns, sooner or later, to very much the same place. Did the Lowsons swim?'

'Oh, not that day, I'm sure. I don't know about any other day, but they'd only come down that same afternoon. I found them there when I got back after dining in Stack Ferry.'

'And you saw nobody on the marshes or the shore that night except your companion, Miss St John?'

'I thought I had answered that. I saw nobody until I was back in my car and was ready to drive off. Then I thought I saw somebody wearing white, but the thing was quite a long way off.'

'All the same, by moonlight it is still possible to recognise a figure, if not a face.'

'I was mistaken in what I thought. The person I thought it might have been was no longer wearing white that evening. All I saw was marsh mist.'

Dame Beatrice did not press the point.

CHAPTER 13

INTERIM

'Hence! home, you idle creatures,
get you home: Is this a holiday?'
William Shakespeare

When Dame Beatrice returned to her home it was to find her secretary there. She greeted Laura warmly, but added: 'I did not expect you back so soon.'

'Oh, Gavin was called upon at short notice to attend an Interpol conference in West Germany. It seemed pointless to stay on without him, so here I am, filled with the London ozone of lead poisoning and petrol fumes, and with a heart for any fate, as the Master of English Prose so often said. You didn't tell me much about it in your letters, but I gather you've been busy on a case of murder.'

'That it is a case of murder has not been proved. There is every likelihood that it never *will* be proved.' She gave Laura a brief but sufficient account of her activities concerning the death of Camilla Hoveton St John.

'So this Palgrave mentioned blackmail, did he?' said Laura. 'He's a schoolmaster, you say – Caesar's wife, in other words. Wonder whether the girl had anything to go on?'

'Before I left him we discussed the matter. He did not believe the girl would have carried out her threat and he assured me that there was nothing in her insinuations and that she withdrew them on the plea that she had been joking. Apparently he threatened her that his union would sue her for defamation of character.'

'Yes, well, it's not the sort of joke a man who teaches in a mixed comprehensive, where the kids stay on until they're seventeen or eighteen, would find very funny. I think, on the face of it, that he's your murderer.'

'He may be the chief, but he is not the only suspect. The girl seems to have involved herself with other men while she was living in the cottage. So far as Mr Palgrave is concerned, I gave him every chance to tell me some easy lies, but he did not avail himself of the opportunity.'

'Oh, yes? Clever enough to see the snares you were laying, perhaps.'

'Yes, but it must have been a temptation to take an obvious way out. He must know that he is the chief suspect, so I gave him the opportunity of saying that he was not the only member of the cottage party who was out of the house that night. He did not take advantage of this. He agreed that Mrs Lowson was out walking, but he was compelled to admit this as others, of course, can testify to it. Besides, on the face of it, she appears to be the last person to have needed to lay violent hands upon Miss St John, since she had met her for the first time that day.'

'What about the husband?'

'Cupar Lowson? He is well out of it, it seems. He was in bed, presumably asleep, at the time when Palgrave left the cottage to drive to Stack Ferry that night. Palgrave saw him.'

'Palgrave said Lowson was in bed?'

'Palgrave said so. My suggestion that both the Lowsons and both the Kirbys may have been out he ignored. As Mrs Kirby told me that Miss St John had attempted to seduce Adrian Kirby, I thought that Mr Palgrave might have risen to my bait, but he did not.'

'So exit Palgrave and all's well?'

'By no means. I mention the matter for what it is worth. The difficulty is that if none of the cottage party was involved, that brings us to the need to consider an incalculable number of outsiders. The place was teeming with yachtsmen and other summer visitors and the girl was avid for male society. Further to that, but for the mysterious business of the suitcase, as I explained to you, there is little reason to think that the verdict at the inquest was mistaken.'

'That the girl swam on an outgoing tide and was drowned because she couldn't get back to shore? As a swimmer myself, I still can't swallow that. Mind you, if she was the kind of little tramp you indicate, and some man was there, egging her on, well, she *might* have been daft enough to do it, I suppose.'

'I think the possibilities have all been considered and I am inclined to reject that one.'

'There is just one thing,' said Laura. 'When Palgrave admitted that Lowson was in bed and asleep that night, was that both when he entered the cottage and when he left it?'

'He seems to have assumed that it was both. Palgrave was in the cottage for about half an hour. He groped around for his suitcase, went upstairs to change his clothes, went into the kitchen to shave and straight out to his car when he had done this.'

'Why should he go upstairs to change?'

'Not to disturb the sleeping man.'

'I don't believe he would have bothered about that. Do you know what I think? I think that when Palgrave nipped in and groped around for his suitcase, he assumed that *both* the Lowsons were asleep in bed. It was only when he was leaving that he discovered that Lowson was on his own in the room.'

'You may be right. I wonder why Mr Lowson did not accompany his wife on her moonlight walk? One would have thought that in a strange environment he would have been anxious to be with her.'

'They may have had a bit of a toss-up and she was walking it off while he preferred to fume and sulk in bed.'

'What an imaginative mind you have!'

'Another possibility is that Lowson murdered the girl and sneaked back while Palgrave was upstairs or in the kitchen. Anyway, there could be a simple explanation for the girl's suitcase being found on the dunes.'

'In what way?'

'You said that Palgrave took the others to the pub that night. They probably didn't bother to lock up before they went. People don't, in the country. Couldn't a thief have oiled in, pinched the girl's suitcase and hidden it among the sand-dunes until he could sell it and her clothes?'

'There are objections to that theory. It assumes that the intruder knew that the cottage was empty. If so, there was nothing to prevent a thief from looking around to find something worth stealing. Surely the holiday clothes of Dr Lowson and his wife, not to mention those of Mr Palgrave, would have been better worth taking than Miss St John's admittedly small and dingy little outfit?'

'Perhaps he didn't think he had much time. As I see it, he would have popped in and out as quickly as he could.'

'Then why go upstairs when there were three suitcases to hand just inside the front door? Even if Mr Palgrave is lying, and his own suitcase was already in the boot of his car, there were still the Lowsons' things ready for the picking up. Even if he did risk going upstairs, why choose Miss St John's — '

'Tatty little outfit in preference to the Lowsons' kit? Very well, then. Pass, theory that there could have been a thief, although to my mind it is still a possibility which ought to be taken into account if no other evidence is forthcoming. But, surely, so far as you've gone, doesn't everything point to Palgrave? There's no doubt he bathed with the girl that night, he came back to the cottage knowing she wouldn't be there, and his rather feeble story seems to have been that he "left her in the sea". Well, she had not only made a perfect nuisance of herself to him, but had actually threatened (jokingly or not) to blackmail him. Add to this the fact that, instead of sleeping in his car as he had said he had intended doing, he admits that he drove around in the small hours until he found a café where he could get breakfast. Then he went to the hotel at Stack Ferry and took up his reservation earlier than he had intended. Sounds very fishy to me.'

'And may well be so, I agree, although, of course, hotels do take customers mid-week.'

'Then, since you are convinced there was murder done, why do you think I'm wrong?'

'I would not say – in fact, I have not said – that you are wrong. Moreover, you have made a most valuable suggestion, although it had already occurred to me.'

Time passed. The holiday season ended. The yachtsmen laid up their boats, the holiday cottages were vacated, the hotels paid off their auxiliary staff, the beaches were almost deserted and melancholy settled over the salt-marshes. The creeks and channels on the east side of Stack Ferry were left to the densely packed colonies of crustacean-eating knots and the winter visitors, including wild geese, mallard, teal, wild duck, widgeon and the predatory wild-fowler who was licensed to shoot them. Dame Beatrice, after exploring such avenues as remained open in the case of Camilla, decided to settle down to an autumn routine and the business of getting Christmas out of the way and hoping, with Mr Micawber, that something would turn up.

Laura said no more about the death and might have been excused for thinking that Dame Beatrice had lost all interest in the case. She knew her employer too well, however, to suppose anything of the kind.

Palgrave returned to his classroom and its puerilities and when the school closed for a week at the half-term holiday at the end of October, he booked himself in again at The Stadholder with the proviso that he be allotted a better room than his previous little attic and one with facilities for his writing. This, he felt, was going extremely well. As soon as the chores of marking exercise books and preparing for the following day's lessons were done with, he had accustomed himself to a discipline of writing until one in the morning. His weekends, except for a Sunday round of golf with a colleague, were similarly devoted to his novel and his pile of typescript was becoming encouragingly high.

At Stack Ferry he took daily exercise by walking towards Saltacres and, rather to his own surprise, one morning he felt impelled to drive into the little town where the house agent lived and book the cottage of which he had such traumatic memories, proposing to spend the three weeks of his Christmas holiday there, although where the impulse came from which prompted him to do this, he did not know. All the descriptions of the scenery that he needed were already down on paper, he thought.

He told himself that he was merely trying to avoid having to spend Christmas in London, but he found this reason strangely unconvincing. Miranda sent him, at the beginning of December, an invitation for Boxing Day, and he was glad that he had a legitimate reason for refusing it. He wrote that he would be away for the whole of the Christmas holiday, but something prevented him from telling her where he was going.

School broke up on the eighteenth of December. He loaded the boot of the car with the provision he had made for

Christmas fare as well as with the more day to day tins of meat, fish, biscuits and vegetables he would need, and on the Saturday he set out blithely on his hundred-mile journey.

There were no problems. He lunched early at a pub outside Cambridge and reached Saltacres well before dusk, early though the sun set at that time of year.

He had schooled himself to believe that there might be some haunted quality about the cottage when he had it all to himself, but this was disproved as soon as, with the key for which he had called at the house agent's on his way up, he let himself in. Except that the place seemed smaller, darker, dingier and damper than he remembered it, all seemed familiar and reassuring.

Having dumped his luggage and unloaded his provisions, he parked his car in the accustomed place a little further up the street, returned to the cottage, lit the gas fire in the parlour and then made an investigation upstairs in order to decide upon his sleeping-quarters. He had never been inside the larger bedroom, but as soon as he looked at it he favoured it.

He went into what had been Camilla's room, but it evoked no painful memories. Downstairs the studio couch, well-worn but offering no suggestion that it could also do duty as a bed – and Morag's bed, at that! – and his little work-table still in the window, were reminders of the previous holiday, but he experienced no traumatic reaction. He unpacked his typescript and placed it on the parlour table, put his portable typewriter beside it, drew the curtains and lit the gas-mantle. Then he got himself a meal and afterwards finished the evening at the warm and friendly pub.

'This is the life,' he said to himself, and had thoughts of throwing up his job at the end of the summer term, buying the cottage, if the agent would sell, and living on his savings plus a little assistance, perhaps, from an indulgent government while he blossomed out into full, professional authorship.

In the morning, after breakfast, he went out for the walk he had decided to take daily for exercise, but, after a couple of miles, the biting wind made walking so unpleasant that he was glad to return to the cottage for the rest of the day. During the night the wind dropped and the snow fell. He woke to a shining, white-blanketed, silent world. Gone were the wild wastes of the marshes as he had seen them. The apparently illimitable wilderness was still there, but the alchemy of the snow had changed it into something so rich and strange that he was awed by it and, at the same time, he was filled with the liveliest anticipation and delight.

He stepped out of the cottage feeling like the first man on the moon, and tramped over the crisp, virgin purity of the snow with the pleasure of a child who recognises the magic of his own footprints.

'I never thought of *snow* for chapter ten,' he said aloud. He returned to the cottage and settled down to record this new phenomenon of an enchanted, utterly unexpected world. 'Just what I needed, and I never thought of it!' he repeated joyously.

He continued to take his morning exercise, but his walks grew shorter every day. No more snow fell, but what was there remained. He worked on his book from nine until half past twelve each morning, then got himself some lunch and after he had washed up his plates, cutlery and the glass he had used, he went for a short drive more for the sake of the car than because he wanted a change of scene and occupation. After that, it was back to his work again to check over the morning's output and to make any corrections, alterations and embellishments which seemed necessary. He did not think he had ever been so happy.

His evenings he spent at the pub. A couple of pints was his self-imposed ration, and he made them last, his ear alert for any tit-bits of conversation or news which might be worthy of inclusion in the *opus*.

The days passed quickly. On Christmas Day he went to church. It was the first time he had ever been inside the building. Its size was a tribute to a bygone age when the village had been a prosperous township and port, and the congregation at this latter day was almost ludicrously small, although he assumed that it was larger than on any other occasion except at the pagan festival of thanksgiving for the harvest.

Like the church at Stack Ferry, this one proclaimed its former trade relations with the Netherlands by its dedication to St Nicholas, the Dutch Santa Claus. Palgrave spent most of the service by taking in, surreptitiously but fully, the hammerbeam and arch-braced roof, its traceried spandrils and flowers, the dropped window-sill of the sedilia in the south wall at the end of the chancel, the Easter sepulchre and the Stuart communion table. The chancel, he noted, was a couple of centuries earlier than the vast and columned nave.

The church must certainly go into his book, he decided. He indulged in a daydream. He and his heroine – he had made her a fascinating combination (he thought) of Morag and Camilla – should marry his hero (himself, Colin) in this most suitable edifice. He sat back in his pew and reflected on what might have been.

The vicar did not detain his small congregation very long. By twelve the Christmas service was over. There were half a dozen misericords under the choir stalls. Palgrave inspected them, but hardly thought they compared with others he had seen at Ripon, Wells, York and Christchurch, let alone the later, more sophisticated and sometimes extremely explicit examples he had seen in French churches. However, he had enjoyed his Christmas morning, for he felt he now had another chapter for his book.

He joined the men of the village in the holly-decked, paper-chained pub before returning to the cottage for his tinned ham and tinned chicken. Then he roughed out a simple marriage ceremony which was to take place in the church, now to be incorporated in a later chapter of his book, and after that he went for a drive over the still snowbound countryside. On the following evening he drove to the most expensive hotel in Stack Ferry for the Boxing Night dinner-dance which he had booked. He was almost struck dumb when Cupar Lowson and Morag came up to his table and suggested that he should join them at theirs.

'Cupar doesn't dance,' said Morag, as though this explained everything. She looked delightful, he thought. He was glad that the fifth and sixth-form girls had insisted upon teaching him the South American style of dancing so that he could stand up with them at school end-of-term parties, but he was better pleased when the hotel orchestra put on some sentimental waltz tunes. It went to his head a little to have Morag in his arms again. He ordered champagne. The other two were staying in the hotel, so neither he nor they left the scene until the dinner-dance closed down at two in the morning.

He drove back to his cottage in moonlight. The effect, over the snow-covered marshes, was fantastic and disturbing. Camilla's ghost must be out there somewhere, he thought. He took his mind back to Morag. The utterly unexpected meeting with her had been equally fantastic and disturbing, especially as it had followed so quickly upon his daydreams in the church.

He began to believe that there was something strange about the book he was writing. Something or somebody was doing the job for him. Suddenly he found he did not like the thought of something which was beyond his control. The book was writing its own story, and not the story he had in his notebook.

He reached his cottage, went in and poured himself a drink. Then he took out the script and had a look at it. With what he recognised as a superstitious reaction, he crossed himself, put the script away and went to bed. In the morning he took his book out again and this time his reaction was different. He began to read and, as he read, he said aloud, 'But this is damn' good stuff. *Damn'* good. Morag is going to like this when I show it to her.'

CHAPTER 14

THE FLAT-MATES

'Thoughts, like old vultures, prey upon their heart-strings.'
Isaac Watts

Meanwhile, as Laura had surmised, Dame Beatrice had by no means lost interest in the case. She was still curious about Camilla's death by drowning, was challenged by the doubts and difficulties concerning it and decided that the most obvious approach to a solution of the problem was to find out more about the girl herself and the kind of life she had led before her disastrous visit to Saltacres.

Her first move was to contact Adrian and Miranda again in the early autumn and make an attempt to get them to tell her more about Camilla than she had gained from them so far. She rang them up and invited them to come and stay at the Stone House for a few days. Having received a surprised and pleased acceptance of this offer, she sent her car and her chauffeur to transport them from their London flat to the Stone House.

They brought their paraphernalia with them. She had suggested this.

'Life is quiet here. You will be glad of something to do during your stay.'

So Adrian wandered happily in the woods and over the open stretches of the Forest picking up leaves and fungi and making a collection of beetles. He made what, to him, were delightful discoveries – the brilliant orange colour of the *phlebia* which he found on dead boughs of birch, oak and alder. He came upon a great spotted slug with snail-like horns and obese, mottled body, climbing the cap of *amanita rubescens* (known to country people as the Blusher because of its pink stain), and made a beautiful and delicate sketch which he gave to Laura. He found the elegant but poisonous wood blewit and liked the colour of the blue cap which gave it its name the Amethyst, and made another colour sketch for Dame Beatrice.

The Verdigris toadstool, named for the violet *laccaria*, and the charming little *marismius rotula*, the Fairy Umbrella, he sketched for his own use. Wild flowers were hard to find at that time of year, for it was September, but he found ling and some sweetly scented dodder on the open heathland, and the common gorse was here and there in flower.

'Adrian is so happy,' said Miranda. 'I'm glad the weather is fine. I wonder whether you will accept my picture of your garden? It has made a change from my usual work.'

It was after dinner each evening that they talked about Camilla. Dame Beatrice listened attentively to the small anecdotes, mostly connected with the art school which was the venue where Miranda had usually encountered Camilla before they had taken her to Saltacres.

'She was too casual in her attitude to her work ever to become first class. She had talent, but she dissipated it. She frivolled away her time and then, of course, this everlasting chasing after men when, poor girl, she was not even attractive to them, did her work nothing but harm. Work must come first, and a long way first, if it is to win recognition,' said Miranda.

Dame Beatrice enquired about fees at the art school.

'Oh, the fees are reasonable enough,' said Miranda.

'It is the materials which cost the money,' said Adrian. 'Somebody once said that the best poetry is written on good paper with a good pen – or words to that effect – and the same theory applies even more closely to painting. If the materials are not up to standard, the results cannot be anything but disappointing.'

'Could Miss St John afford good materials?' Dame Beatrice enquired.

'Oh, yes, those she used were quite adequate,' Miranda responded. 'She worked in an art dealer's and picture-frame maker's shop before she became a full-time art student, so she may have been able to get a discount.'

'I should doubt that, once she had stopped working for them,' said Adrian.

THE FLAT-MATES

'I believe I have been told that she had a private income,' said Dame Beatrice. 'Do you know whether she ever made a Will?'

'I should think it extremely unlikely,' said Miranda. 'Are you suggesting that somebody murdered her for her money? I don't believe she had all that much, you know. She dressed sloppily and cheaply—'

'I don't believe that is anything to go by in these days,' said Adrian. 'They all buy cheaply and then throw away. *Mending* is a dirty word with teenagers.'

'Well, it's hardly a romantic occupation,' said his wife, 'as you would know if you had to do it.'

'When did Miss St John come into her inheritance and give up her employment, I wonder?' said Dame Beatrice. Neither of the couple could remember the date on which she had enrolled at the art school, but Adrian promised to call at the place where Camilla had worked – he knew the shop and patronised it occasionally – and Miranda volunteered to produce the other information.

This was all the help they could offer, but when they got home they kept their word and did more than they had promised. Camilla had given in her notice at the shop some year and a half before she had accompanied the Kirbys to Saltacres, and she had registered as an art student at the beginning of the autumn term after her notice at the shop had expired. She received a discount on her own purchases whenever she brought another customer along, but the discount was very small.

'One other thing I did,' wrote Adrian in his small, neat, masculine hand, 'was to ask about her Will. It does not appear to exist. I tried under Hoveton and all the other Johns and St Johns, and I also tried, of course, under her real name of Thomasina Smith.'

'I don't think I have heard that name before,' said Dame Beatrice over the telephone when she thanked him for his letter and all the trouble he had taken.

'She wasn't proud of it. That's why she changed it, but they knew her by it at the shop,' said Adrian. 'I'm sorry we've been of so little help.'

'That is not true. I shall now go and see whether her

flat-mates can add anything to what you have told me. You gave me the address – or, rather, your wife did. I will write straight away to Miss Minehart.'

Gerda Minehart's answer came promptly, proving that artists can be businesslike. It was a lengthy letter. The writer had always been in touch with the Kirbys, since she and they had much in common, and, having heard Miranda's account of Camilla's death, she was completely mystified by it (she wrote) and would welcome a visit from Dame Beatrice, and so would the others with whom she shared the flat.

The flat turned out to be misnamed. It was not literally a flat at all, as it was on two floors. The lower one of these had been turned into a large studio which was shared by all four women. Above it were the four bed-sitting-rooms, one of which had already been let to another artist in place of Camilla. As she also had been acquainted with the dead girl, she was anxious to take part in the conference.

This took place on a Saturday, when the school was closed so far as the art classes were concerned, but open for students who wanted to put in some extra time there – chiefly, Gerda Minehart explained, the potters and sculptors, as the building offered facilities which many of the students did not possess in their homes or lodgings.

Dame Beatrice expected little to come of the visit so far as any explanation of Camilla's death was concerned, but she found the flat-mates interesting. From Miranda's description, she had no difficulty in identifying the three who had actually shared the premises with Camilla, even before the introductions were made.

Gerda Minehart was not only the oldest but the undoubted leader of the little group, and it was in her bed-sitter that the meeting was held. She was Jewish and while she was dispensing hospitality in the form of tea and cake she mentioned the name of Conradda Mendel.

'She has often spoken of you,' she said.

'Yes, she was once connected with a case I was called upon to look into,' said Dame Beatrice. She gazed at the one picture in the room, a spirited study of a horse being shod. 'She also assists me to choose what to buy in the sale rooms from time to time when I am moved to acquire a modest item or two of antique silverware.'

'She acts as my agent, too,' said Gerda, 'but on the other side of the fence. She negotiates the sale of my pictures – on a commission basis, of course. This ensures that she does her best for me.' She followed the direction of Dame Beatrice's eyes. 'That's one of my things.'

'It is splendid.'

'Yes, it is,' the artist agreed without boastfulness but with the solid satisfaction of a master craftsman acknowledging quite impersonally the feeling for a job well done. The other three made apporpriate murmurs of agreement. The socialite Mevagissey, whose first name, it appeared, was Claire and whose signature to her pictures was 'in honour,' she informed Dame Beatrice, 'of the most ravishing little fishing port on earth, for Mevagissey, of course, is not my surname,' fingered a necklace of jade as she listened and talked.

'Ah, you paint fishing-boats and seascapes,' said Dame Beatrice.

'So did Camilla, when she went to the seaside with Miranda and Adrian,' said the beautiful, voluptuous Fenella, leaning back in her chair and yawning. 'It doesn't seem the healthiest of subjects to choose, does it, if one gets drowned in the end?'

'Well, that's one way of looking at it,' said the newly joined member of the group. 'But what I think—'

'Has no significance, Val, darling,' said Gerda. 'Fenella, in her elephantine way – all right, Fen! Don't bother to aim your bosom at me! You've done us a favour by bringing up the subject Dame Beatrice wants to talk about. What do you want us to tell you about Camilla, Dame Beatrice?'

'How many people knew that she was going to Saltacres with Mr and Mrs Kirby?'

'I should think anybody at the art school could have known,' said Mevagissey. 'There was nothing secret about it. Miranda usually took one or even two of the students with her and Adrian when they went away in the summer.'

'Do you know of anybody who would wish to harm her?'

'Again, there could be any number,' said Gerda, 'but they wouldn't murder her, you know. Nobody took her seriously enough for that.'

'She swiped their boyfriends, though,' said the youthful Valerie.

'Not mine,' said Fenella complacently, 'and the men didn't stay swiped very long. They soon began looking for something a bit more beddable.'

'She really was her own worst enemy, I expect,' said Mevagissey, 'and, as you say, she never managed to keep the boyfriends after she'd stolen them. They soon tired of her. She was a bit of a laughing stock actually.'

'She was a little rat. I wonder anybody was ever tempted to sample her,' said Fenella.

'Anyway, nobody would have bothered to murder her,' said Gerda again.

'Would she ever have contemplated suicide, I wonder?' asked Dame Beatrice.

'Oh, no!' said Valerie and Mevagissey together.

'No,' said Fenella. 'She enjoyed life in her own way, poor little sod.'

'I don't think she minded losing her men after she'd collected them,' said Gerda. 'It was the chase she liked.'

'But what of the deprived young women?' Dame Beatrice enquired.

'Oh, Camilla wasn't the only predator,' said Fenella. 'People are always changing their sleeping partners. Nobody we know would murder anybody because of a swap-over of bodies, otherwise we'd all be in Kensal Green by now.'

'Do you know anything of her background – her parentage, education, that sort of thing? Her real name appears to have been Smith. There seems to be no evidence that she herself ever made a Will, but presumably her father or another relative left her something, or she would not have been in a position to give up her paid employment and live on a private income.'

Fenella and Claire Mevagissey exchanged glances and Gerda, Dame Beatrice thought, looked troubled. Nobody spoke until Valerie said, 'We've wondered about that ourselves.'

'Better not talk,' said Gerda. 'We don't *know* anything.'

'You can't libel the dead,' said Fenella.

'You can blacken their memory.'

'Her reputation wasn't all *that* shiny.'

'This,' said Dame Beatrice, 'is an enquiry into what I am convinced was a case of murder. Anything you may tell me or the police will be held to be entirely confidential unless it is needed as evidence in a court of law.' She looked at each one of them in turn. It was Fenella who spoke.

'We always thought she had managed to get somebody on a piece of string,' she said. 'We – Gerda and Claire and I – were at a party with her. She got pretty high and she, well, let a rather big cat out of the bag when we got her home. I don't suppose she remembered afterwards what she'd said. She had been too much under the influence to remember anything much at all, I guess.'

'She was just full of wild babble,' said Gerda. 'She didn't know what she was talking about.'

'They do, you know,' retorted Fenella. 'They know perfectly well what they're talking about until they actually go under the ether, and by the time they wake up, complete with hangover, they haven't the blindest conception of what they've let out and nobody is more surprised than themselves if someone repeats it to them.'

'But you did not repeat it to her, I imagine,' said Dame Beatrice.

'Heavens, no! It was none of our business if she was putting the screw on somebody.'

'Man or woman, I wonder?'

'She didn't say, but we thought, knowing Camilla and her ways, that it was a man and probably not one of our gang at all, but somebody who couldn't afford *not* to pay up. The inference was that she'd collected a little bundle, and that this evidence was still available to earnest enquirers, and that it would be pretty serious for the man if somebody talked.'

'This would have happened while she was still employed at the shop, I take it, otherwise you would not need to *infer*, because you would *know*, if she had been living here at the time.'

'Well— ' Fenella and Mevagissey exchanged glances again. 'Well— only *sort* of while she was still at the shop, if you know what I mean,' said Fenella.

'She had to go to hospital,' said Claire.

'I am accustomed to reading between the lines.' Dame Beatrice rose to go. 'Thank you all for your help. You have clarified my own ideas to a most gratifying extent. Blackmail is a particularly nasty business.'

Gerda accompanied her downstairs.

'I don't believe Camilla had a baby,' she said. 'She was far too fly to go so far as that.'

'She was not fly enough to avoid being murdered,' said Dame Beatrice.

'People shouldn't write or do things for which they can be blackmailed. It's their own fault if somebody takes advantage of them and cashes in.'

'What did you really think of Miss St John?'

'I was sorry for her. She was all the time chasing the bluebird and every time she caught it it died on her.'

'But the dog it was that died,' said Dame Beatrice.

'The little bitch, you mean. Oh, she was that, all right,' said Gerda, 'and we're pretty sure about the blackmail, although we don't know any names.'

CHAPTER 15

THE MUDFLATS, LONDON RIVER

'It's a long, long watch that he's a-keeping there,
And a dead cold night that lays a-creeping there.'
Henry Newbolt

Briefed by Dame Beatrice when she returned to the hotel which they used when they were staying only a day or two in London, Laura went to the art dealer's shop which the Kirbys had mentioned. She was armed with a list of requisites consisting of light-to-carry articles such as charcoal, paint brushes, a small sketching block and some varnish and Dame Beatrice had also prepared for her a series of questions to put to the proprietor.

She was served by an auburn-haired girl of Burne-Jones aspect while a man whom Laura took to be the person she had come to question was busy with another customer. She gave her order with many pauses to consult a piece of paper on which she had written down the items she intended to purchase. The pauses were to gain as much time as she could in the hope that the shopkeeper himself would soon be free.

Halfway through her list and while she was still playing for time, she said:

'You're not the one who served me about a couple of years ago, are you?'

'Hardly,' said the girl. 'I've only been here six months.'

'Ah,' said Laura, inspecting the brushes which had been placed before her, 'that would account for it. I'll take, yes, this and this — or shall I? — perhaps — well, what do you think?'

'It depends what you want them for. I mean, the kind of picture and the size of it, and whether you're a splasher or a niggler, I suppose.'

'Yes, I suppose it would. I'm not buying for myself, you see, but for somebody who is elderly and finds shopping difficult.'

'Surely he told you the numbering of the brushes he wants?'

'He's only an amateur. Dabbles about just to have something to do, you know.'

'You're his nurse, are you?'

'Oh, general factotum,' said Laura, trying to imagine Dame Beatrice needing a nurse. At this moment the other customer left and the proprietor came up to them.

'Can I help?' he enquired.

'The lady is shopping for somebody else and isn't quite sure what is wanted,' said the girl.

'Oh, well, I'll take over, Miss Wareham, if you'll attend to the customer who has just come in.'

Laura completed her purchases under his advice and then said:

'You used to have an assistant named Smith – Thomasina Smith – about two years ago.'

'Certainly. She had to go into hospital and left shortly after she was discharged.'

'*You* didn't discharge her from your shop?'

'She preferred to discharge herself. She still shops here occasionally. She is quite a casual visitor, though.'

'A casual visitor?' said Laura. 'I wonder what you mean by that?'

'She came at intervals. It is some weeks, I believe, since we saw her. She brings us purchasers, of course.'

'Apart from what I feel sure you have indicated with regard to her character and general demeanour— '

'Please, please! You are not a woman police constable, are you?'

'No, no. Why should you ask that?'

'Because Miss Smith has not called here for some time. I wondered whether she was in trouble with the police.'

'Well,' said Laura, 'why should *you* care?'

'I do not care. She was a very immoral young woman. She had to go into hospital, and I had good reason to be glad for her to leave. She was not a desirable employee. And now I am sorry, but I've got a customer, if you'll excuse me.'

'Right. Thanks for your help. I'm sure my employer will like the brushes and things.'

'We have a long list of satisfied customers, I am glad to say.'

Laura went back to Dame Beatrice, wondering, as she went, whether the art dealer knew more about Camilla's death than he could be expected to admit.

'How went your errand?' Dame Beatrice enquired.

'Only so-so. Anyway, it's a very good shop, two large front windows, some decent originals and some very good copies on display and so many different kinds of artists' materials that beshrew me if I don't start up in the plaster, dab and palette knife routine myself, come the long winter evenings.'

'Woodcarving would suit you, but tell me about the interview.'

'I soft pedalled, as you told me, and two things emerged. The man has no idea that Thomasina Smith and Camilla Hoveton St John are one and the same, for he still talks of her in the present tense. He certainly hasn't a clue about the death, unless he has become suspect number one.'

'Is that really the impression you received?'

'Well, no, it isn't, but there's no doubt about two things. The girl did not go into hospital because of a car crash or any accident of that sort. He turned very cagey, as a matter of fact, about the hospital angle. I suspected she went into a maternity ward or had an abortion. One thing he did make clear. If she had not given in her notice at his shop, she would have been sacked.'

'Her notice, yes,' said Dame Beatrice. 'According to the artists with whom she shared an apartment, she was able to give up paid employment only because she was blackmailing somebody.'

'And the somebody turned nasty and made away with her? Do you think there is any point in pursuing the thing any further?'

'Probably no point at all. The women in the flat have no proof of what they told me, anybody at the art school could have known that the girl was to spend a fortnight's holiday with the Kirbys, and I do not suppose that Mrs Kirby made any secret of the fact that the holiday was to be spent at Saltacres. The girl herself may have told her murderer where she would be.'

'Leaves a big field to cover.'

'I will let the police know of the rumour that blackmail could be involved and then, unless some bit of clear evidence turns up, which seems unlikely after all this time, I shall sit back and allow the police to solve the problem, or not, as they see fit.'

Laura looked at the sharp black eyes and beaky little mouth and said,

'I believe that in your own mind the problem is already solved.'

'Yes,' said Dame Beatrice, 'in my own mind it is, but there is not a shred of proof. Besides, I dislike blackmail and I always feel sympathy for a worm which has the courage to turn.'

'All the same, you can't be blackmailed unless you've done something silly or naughty, can you?'

'True. Well, to other matters. We have several invitations to spend Christmas with relatives and friends. What are your plans?'

'Paris with Hamish, and Hogmanay with Eiladh and Tom, unless you want me with you.'

'You are included in my invitations, of course.'

'Thanks, but Gavin thinks he can snaffle a few days at the beginning of January.'

'Then I shall go to Carey in Oxfordshire.'

'You wouldn't like to give me a hint about our murderer, would you?'

'No.'

The weeks passed. Christmas, and Palgrave's unexpected meeting with Morag and Cupar Lowson, came and went. By the middle of January both Dame Beatrice and Laura were settled down again in the Stone House and the vexed subject of Camilla's death was not raised again by either of them. One pale, early spring morning, Dame Beatrice, coming into the room her secretary used as an office, said:

'Authors are the most egoistic of human beings, with the possible exception of politicians.'

'You're thinking of Palgrave?'

'In more ways than one. He has telephoned me about this book he has written. He calls it a psychological treatise in the form of a novel and would like my blessing on it.'

'You'll have to write him a preface, then, if you agree to

sponsor the thing. It's a bit of a cheek for him to ask you. Shall you do it?'

'Not until I have read the book, of course. Tomorrow morning we will draft a reply.'

'May be too late,' said Laura bluntly.

'I wonder what you mean?'

'I don't know what I mean. Maybe we shall both know when we have read the book. Have you seen the evening paper?'

'No. Why?' Dame Beatrice looked curiously at her secretary.

'The mudflats appear to have claimed another victim,' said Laura.

'At Saltacres?'

'No, at low tide on the Thames.'

The entrance to the small up-river docks was being dredged. The dredger was an old one of the bucket type and had a squat, black, filthy-looking hopper alongside. As the work went on, bucket after bucket of slimy mud, stones and an incredible assortment of river debris came up and was deposited in the hopper.

The docks were at the confluence of the river and a canal and served as a short-time repository for the goods brought on the canal boats from the Midlands, and as a temporary warehouse for the cargoes to be carried north again.

Although a dead man lay out on the mud a hundred yards away, the four men working on the dredger did not notice him; neither did the occasional stroller along the path on the opposite side of the river. There were willows on that side and, further to that, the banks were high and had been shored up with sacks of concrete and the dead man was lying too far in, where the high tide had left him, to be visible to any casual walker who did not go right up to the edge of the bank and peer over.

The person who first spotted him was the youthful cox of a pair-oar racing skiff who was out early practising with his two-man crew for the local Easter regatta. As the skiff was undergoing a time trial over what was to be the course on the great day, he said nothing of his discovery until the skiff was being paddled back to the boathouse.

'Go easy and pull over to the Surrey side when we gets to the dredger,' he said to his brothers. 'I reckon I seen a stiff laying out on the mud.'

His rowers were sceptical, but he soon proved himself to be right. They could not take their frail craft up to the edge of the river, for fear of damaging her, but even from twenty yards out there could be no doubt that, fairly close under the bank, lay a very dead man. He was fully clothed, even to the extent of wearing an overcoat, although his head was bare.

'Dead drunk, and fell in and the tide took him,' said bow oar as they paddled downstream.

'Suicided hisself, poor b—,' said stroke. 'Lots does it in the river.' The youthful cox said,

'Means the police, anyway. I got to go to school and, anyway, they wouldn't take no notice of me, so one of you better tell 'em.'

'We'll get Dad to do it. He's the one with the spare time. We got to get to bloody work,' said bow oar.

'Tell 'im it might be a murder. That'll be meat and drink to Dad. Loves his murders. Sunday paper lasts him all day and Monday as well,' said stroke. 'Besides, he knows the Sergeant.'

'Been dead a couple of days or more,' said the police surgeon. 'Who is he?'

'Nothing to show,' said the local Superintendent of Police. 'No papers, no wallet, nothing to identify him at present. Have to be an autopsy before the inquest, I suppose, just in case.'

'In case he's been mugged and murdered? You're quite right, of course, to investigate,' said the doctor, 'although it looks a straight case of suicide to me. Clothes seem quite good. Well-kept body, too, well-nourished and clean. Age somewhere around thirty, at a guess. All his own teeth and well-tended hands and feet. Professional class I should think. Not a manual worker, anyway. Who found him?'

'Three young lads out rowing. They told their father that the kid acting as cox had spotted him on the foreshore mud when they were out for early morning practice, and the old man came along and made a report. I've got their names and the address. Locals. Practising for the regatta. Well, until somebody comes forward and reports him as missing, it's not going to be easy to identify him. Clothes came from one of those multiple chain stores which sell menswear – Angler Brothers, to be exact – and the shirt was the kind you can buy at any M and S store, socks ditto. The shoes were from Bugloss, who've got a shop in every town in the country and dozens in London alone. We'll probably have to wait till somebody misses him. If it's a suicide, probably nobody will. Half of 'em do it because they're either loners or misfits.'

'Not to worry. Somebody will come forward. It's not as though he was one of the Embankment down-and-outs with nobody to care whether he lived or died. Probably in a job. If so, he'll be missed at work after a day or two.'

This prophecy was fulfilled three days later. The first day on which Palgrave failed to turn up at school without telephoning that he would be unable to take his classes affected nobody but the deputy head, who had to deprive resentful colleagues of their free periods, and these colleagues themselves. The headmaster, who, secure in his sanctum behind his desk, was unaffected by the changes, merely remarked, when Palgrave's unexplained absence was reported to him: 'Not like Palgrave. He must be too ill to get to the telephone.'

'There is a landlady, Headmaster. She could have rung up,' said the deputy head.

'Some people don't think of these things or else can't be bothered. Are his classes catered for?'

'Oh, yes.'

'That's all right, then. I expect we shall hear tomorrow. If not, somebody had better go round there.'

This short conversation took place immediately after Assembly on the Monday morning after the body had been found on the same day. No message came during the afternoon or on the following day. When, after Assembly on the Wednesday, Palgrave was still reported missing, the headmaster was sufficiently concerned to send a junior master, who had a car which was parked in the school playground, to Palgrave's address to make enquiries. He returned with unhelpful news.

'I couldn't get an answer at the house, sir, so I enquired of the neighbours. They told me the landlady was called away last Friday to nurse her mother who lives in Basingstoke and they know nothing at all about Palgrave.'

'We shall have to notify the police and ask them to break in, I suppose,' said the headmaster, discussing the matter with his deputy. 'If the poor fellow is ill in bed with nobody to look after him, matters may be serious.'

He rang up the police station. An inspector came to the school.

'Not reported for duty so far this week, sir? Last seen at your school on last Friday afternoon? I shall have to request you to come down to the station, sir, before we go to the lengths of breaking into a private house.'

'Down to the police station? Whatever for?'

'We've got a photograph we want identified, sir.'

Mystified and not too pleased, the headmaster did as he was asked. The photograph was not pretty, but it was identifiable.

'To make sure, sir, the body having been in the water – there's an autopsy report pending, we understand – I'll have to ask you to identify the clothes the deceased was wearing. Perhaps you would come along again, sir, when we've got them, and see if they tally with your identification of the photograph.'

'I couldn't guarantee to do that, unless the clothes are the ones Palgrave wore to school, Inspector. As the poor fellow seems to have drowned either last Friday night or on the Saturday or Sunday, one of my younger staff would be of more use to you than I shall. Mr Winblow was closer to Palgrave than any other, I think. They played golf together, I believe, and spent weekends together sometimes for this purpose. Winblow doubtless will be more familiar with the contents of Palgrave's wardrobe than I am.'

'Very well, sir.'

Winblow identified first the photograph and then the clothes.

'Do you know of any relatives who ought to be informed, sir?' the Superintendent asked the young man.

'I knew he was an orphan, but I never heard of brothers or sisters, or anybody close to him.'

'Oh, well, there's nobody to get a nasty shock, then. You wouldn't have any idea why he did it, I suppose? — not that it's a criminal offence any more.'

'Did it? Did what? Good Lord! You don't suppose it was anything but an accident, do you?'

'We have every reason – it doesn't matter telling you this, sir, because it will have to come out at the inquest, where we shall want you to repeat your evidence of identification – but we have every reason to believe that it was suicide.'

'But – Palgrave? He wasn't the type! I knew him pretty well. He had no troubles, no worries. He'd just finished his second novel and was all lined up to write a third. Those sort of chaps don't put an end to themselves.'

'I'm afraid the evidence given at the inquest will convince you, sir, that sometimes they do.'

'So it's our old friend arsenic, Bob,' said the Inspector, when Winblow, still expressing disbelief, had left.

'Probably took it in black coffee, the pathologist thinks,' said the Superintendent.

'And then went and chucked himself in the river? I thought the stuff laid you out with pains and vomiting. Would he have been in any state to leave his digs and go for a walk?'

'Wonderful what you can do when you've made up your mind to it. But, if you're right, you see what you're saying, don't you?'

'Well, if I'm saying it, you've already thought of it. But who would want to poison a schoolmaster?'

'Some of the kids, perhaps!'

'Of course,' the Superintendent went on thoughtfully, 'there's quite a chance that he wasn't alone when he took the stuff. He may even have been in somebody else's house and passed out there. If these people (or the woman, if he was out on the tiles) had panicked and decided to get rid of the body, how would that do for an answer?'

'A lot of work for us to get busy on, anyway, but we'll see what the inquest brings out.'

The medical evidence given at the inquest was clear. Judging by the fact that there was no water in the lungs, coupled by the amount of arsenic recovered from the body, Palgrave must have been dead when he was put into the water. The verdict was murder by person or persons unknown, and the inquest was adjourned while the police got to work on the case.

They began by rounding up his landlady, who had returned from Basingstoke and suddenly found herself the centre of attraction among her friends and neighbours. Her own alibi for the earliest and also the latest times at which the arsenic could have been administered was unassailable and she had nothing to say (in spite of her excited loquacity) which helped the enquiry in any way whatever.

'Such a nice, quiet, gentlemanly young man. Never any trouble. Always said when he would be out and whether he needed the key. I never give my tenants a key without they are going to be out too late for me or the maid to be up and about to let them in. Yes, he was my only paying guest at the time. I never like calling them lodgers. It's demeaning to them and to me. Yes, you can question the maid if you wish, but, being as she is my niece, although willing to be referred to as the maid to oblige me and keep up the tone, if you know what I mean, I took her with me down my mother's, so she knows no more than I do what poor Mr Palgrave done or where he went, or who he had into his rooms, for that matter.'

'Hadn't Mr Palgrave the right to be looked after, then, while you were in Basingstoke?' asked the patient C.I.D. man who had been assigned to the case.

'Gentlemen being gentlemen, however gentlemanly,' said the landlady impressively, 'I thought it best not to leave a girl what is still not turned twenty in the house alone with a gentleman, if only for the sake of her own good name, the lady next door being of a prying and enquiring nature and all too apt to think the worst, whether it happens or not.'

'So the chances are that Mr Palgrave was alone in the house that weekend?'

'Chance is a fine thing,' said the landlady somewhat abstrusely. 'He had friends.'

'Ah, now we're getting somewhere. Did they visit him here?'

'There used to be a young lady come a lot at one time. They were an engaged couple. I know that, because I saw the ring on her hand one day when she come here, but that was — oh, a matter of two years ago or more. A young man come sometimes and they played cards or else played golf together, but I don't know of nobody else. If he had other friends – and I reckon he did – *he* went to them; they never come to *him*. And that reminds me. When will you have finished with his rooms? I'm losing money all the time you're keeping them sealed up.'

'I'll just take a look around and take away his papers, and then the rooms are all yours, madam. Is the furniture his?'

'That it's not! I let my apartments fully furnished and everything except the little bureau and his clackety old typewriter is mine.'

There was one piece of evidence from the lady who was of 'a prying and enquiring nature and apt to think the worst, whether it happened or not', for her prying nature had led her to go to her sitting-room window to witness the departure of neighbour and niece on the Friday morning. She had returned to it to see Palgrave, on his return from school, let himself in and (she virtuously stated) she had then gone along to see whether there was anything she could do for him.

'And was there?'

'He thanked me and said not, as he was going out to some friends for the weekend. He was dressed very careful, so I thought there was a lady in the case, but, of course, poor gentleman, he never come back at all and I never seen him again.'

The obvious line of enquiry was to find out where Palgrave had gone on that Friday evening, but his correspondence, as much of it as he seemed to have kept, dealt only with school or with business matters connected with his literary agents, or else it consisted of receipted bills. There was no private correspondence of any kind.

There were his professional certificates and a couple of testimonials from head teachers under whom he had served before he obtained an extra-mural academic degree and his post as senior English master at his last school and there was the signed contract from his publishers. There was also a typed carbon copy of a novel, but he appeared to have kept neither a diary nor an address book.

The detective removed such papers as there were. Some of these supplied the names and addresses of his publishers and his literary agents, one of whose letters regretted 'your decision, which we hope very much that you will reconsider.'

'Wonder what that was?' said the Inspector. 'He hadn't read the letter. I had to slit it open.'

There seemed nothing useful about the papers so far as an explanation of the death was concerned. There was a cheque book with all the counterfoils carefully filled in, and there was a paying-in book hardly used at all, so both of these gave the name of his bank and the suburb in which the branch was housed, but were of no other assistance.

On inspection of the documents and of a recent bank statement which the police also found among his papers, Palgrave appeared to have had no money troubles and his bank manager endorsed this conclusion. Palgrave's salary was paid in automatically and he merely received a monthly pay-slip recording the amount sent to the bank and listing the deductions for tax and insurance. None of it was helpful in tracing his murderer.

The bank manager, in answer to a question, said that he had no idea as to whether Palgrave had ever made a Will. He said he doubted it. Men of Palgrave's age and financial circumstances seldom bothered unless they were married, and not always then.

'Had he any life assurance or any other insurance policies which could mature at his death? We've found nothing of the kind among his papers, but people do keep such things at the bank.'

'I suppose you are looking for a motive,' said the bank manager. 'I know of none. So far as I can see, money wouldn't enter into it. Why don't you get in touch with his Union? He's bound to have belonged to something of the sort. They may be able to help you.'

Palgrave's death was reported in two or three local papers, first as suicide and then, after the inquest, more excitedly and at greater length, as murder. The big dailies took up the story, one of the more sensational sheets heading it *The Golden Treasury Murder,* because of Palgrave's surname. The report came to the notice of Gerda, who showed it to Miranda at the art school and said: 'Didn't you once say you knew a man named Palgrave? Didn't you tell me he stayed with you and Camilla St John when you went on holiday? – and didn't you send that terrifying Dame Beatrice to see us? Well, somebody fed him arsenic and dropped him in the Thames. It tells you all about it here. It seems a funny kind of business to me and I think there must must be a tie-up somewhere with Camilla's death, which we heard about from Dame Beatrice's visit. There's a kind of Greek tragedy feeling about it – mud-flats, and tides carrying bodies about, and no obvious or particular reason for either death.'

'Oh, a number of people might have had reason to wish Camilla dead,' said Miranda. 'I don't know about Colin.'

To Detective-Inspector Pinhurst of the C.I.D., a very bright and up-coming young man, there was one aspect of the case which posed a most interesting problem. Not only had he gone through all Palgrave's papers not once but several times; he had also read the carbon copy of Palgrave's novel, once with a quick skim through, the second time more slowly, thus following the pattern with which he was accustomed to take his drinks when he drank at all.

Going by that instinct (for want of a more accurate word) which was to stand him in excellent stead for the furtherance of a distinguished career, he found himself certain that the key to the mystery of Palgrave's death lay somewhere or other in the contents of the novel.

For one thing, he could not make out why the author had withdrawn the book from publication. Pinhurst was well-read, and the story seemed to him well constructed and well written and to contain no legally objectionable matter whatsoever. He submitted the book to a solicitor well versed in libel cases, and received complete confirmation of his views.

'Even if somebody in the know thought he was one of the characters,' said the lawyer, 'there is nothing which would stand up in the courts and certainly nothing, so far as I can see, which would lead the author to decide to withdraw the book from publication, let alone cause somebody to want him out of the way.'

'All the same,' said Pinhurst, 'I think I'll get a psychologist on to the thing. He may be able to read between the lines and find something which I can't.'

'She, not he,' said the solicitor. 'Dame Beatrice Lestrange Bradley is your answer. She's not only at the top of her profession, but she's the mother of Sir Ferdinand Lestrange, Q.C., and a noted criminologist, attached to the Home Office, at that. Besides, I happen to know that she took an interest in that case of drowning at a place called Saltacres. The girl was found dead on the mudflats there and the mystery of her death has never really been cleared up.'

'There's still a doubt as to whether that was murder, accident or suicide, though, Mr Billington,' said Pinhurst. 'That's how I understood it; whereas there's no doubt about Palgrave. That was murder all right. But I'll certainly contact Dame Beatrice. Further to what you said, her secretary is the Assistant Commissioner's missus, so it's all in the family, so to speak.'

'I can add one more item. Palgrave knew the Hoveton St John girl. I stayed with my brother and another chap at the same place as where the girl got drowned. Dame Beatrice came to us about it and, of course, it was in all the local papers anyway.'

CHAPTER 16

FAINT, BUT PURSUING

'Oh whaur hae ye been, Lord Rendel, my son?
O whaur hae ye been, my sweet pretty one?'
Lord Rendel (Border ballad)

Before contacting Dame Beatrice, Pinhurst said,
'I reckon the first thing to do is to go through this lot again.' He pushed the gleanings from Palgrave's bureau across the desk to his sergeant. 'You take first knock. Damned if *I* can come up with anything from them. If there were large, unaccounted-for sums of money in his bank account, I might suspect he'd been blackmailing somebody and the worm had turned, but there aren't. The book is about blackmail, of course, but so are lots of thrillers.'

'Schoolmasters don't blackmail people, sir. If there was anything of that sort, the boot would be on the other foot, and, anyway, he wouldn't have written about it.'

'Suppose he'd got the goods on a colleague?'

'It's too melodramatic, sir.'

'Well, *you* make a suggestion.'

'A second bank account in another name?'

'But you don't believe in my blackmail theory.'

'I believe in trying anything once, sir, but, no, I can't swallow the blackmail idea, not with a schoolmaster. I'd as soon believe it of a parson.'

'I knew a parson – knew of him, I mean – who was had up for paederasty, so you can't go by a man's calling. The thing is, where do we go from here?'

'I'll make a start on these business letters and bills for the second time of asking, as you suggested, sir. There just *might* be something.'

'Well, if you can find it you're a better man than I am,

Gunga Din. And *that* wouldn't surprise me,' said the Detective-Inspector dispiritedly. 'This is my first case of murder — classical murder, I mean, not pub-brawl stabbings and beating up the Pakis and all that sort of thing — and I'm falling down on it. There doesn't seem to be a lead anywhere.'

The young sergeant got to work on Palgrave's papers and some time later made his report.

'Only one thing strikes me, sir, and I don't suppose it's important. There's a bill here — a receipted bill — from an agency which does typing for authors.'

'Yes, I know. I didn't miss it.'

'Of course not, sir.'

'So what?'

'The bill is for typing a top copy and two carbons of a book called *Lost Parenthesis*.'

'Granted. Don't think much of the title. Wouldn't tempt *me* to pick it up off a bookstall or even off the shelves in a public library, if I hadn't felt bound to read the typescript as being one of the documents.'

'There is also a bill for two photo copies. The thing is — where are they?'

'Oh, they would have been sent off to different publishers, I expect, in hopes that one copy would strike oil. That's the way these authors work, no doubt.'

'But Palgrave wouldn't need to do that sort of thing, sir. He already had a publisher. This was his second book and we've got the original signed contract agreeing to publish his first novel called *If Wishes Were Horses* and calling for an option on another book from him. He wouldn't have needed to go touting for a publisher. No doubt this option book is *Lost Parenthesis*.'

'I still think— oh, no, I don't, though! You're quite right. He had no need to shop around.'

'No, sir, but that's another matter which struck me. There is no letter from the publishers about *Lost Parenthesis* at all. There is the first letter from the literary agents, Peterhead and Peterhead, to say that they've received the typescript and are looking forward to reading it before they pass it on to the publishers, Kent and Weald, but it doesn't look as though Kent and Weald ever received the typescript. I'm wondering whether that other letter from Peterheads, which Palgrave never read because he must have been dead when the landlady put it in his room, was in answer to one of his asking Peterheads not to send Kent and Weald his novel.'

'That sounds a bit strange. I think I'll get on to Peterheads and find out what they're up to. Probably got a lot of scripts to place and haven't got around to reading Palgrave's novel yet. Perhaps, when they do, they'll see why he wanted it withdrawn – if he did!'

'Likely enough, sir, but then there's another thing. He would have sent Peterheads the top copy, no doubt, but that still leaves the photo copies and one of the carbons (there is only one of the carbons among his papers) unaccounted for.'

'Oh, that's easily explained, I think. He probably lent them around among people he thought would read them uncritically and tell him what a genius he was. These writer chaps are all pretty conceited, I expect, especially when they've only had one book published. I remember my nephew getting a letter printed in the *Daily Courier*. Talked about it for weeks. Oh, yes, ten to one he distributed the copies among his friends. I can't see that it matters what he did with them, anyway.'

'No, sir. It just struck me as peculiar, that's all. And there's another thing, sir. Why the photo copies if he already had two carbons?'

'Surely that's an easy one. If his own publisher turned the book down – always a possibility, I suppose – he would need new fresh-looking copies to send to other firms.'

'Then where are they, sir? That was only a carbon we found. You can't mistake a carbon for photo copy. I've done enough typing in this office, sir, to know. I can't help feeling there could be something funny about the other copies, even if a friend has the missing carbon, sir.'

'Well, you'd better go in chase of his friends, then, but I think you'll be wasting your time. Still, we've no other lead. Start with that young fellow from the school. He seems to have known Palgrave pretty well. He may know where he went that Friday evening.'

The headmaster was inclined to be peevish.

'I really must protest, Sergeant,' he said. 'I cannot have my staff harassed in this manner.'

'We are investigating a case of murder, sir.'

'I am fully cognisant of that, but it had nothing to do with my school. I am, of course, horrified that Mr Palgrave should have been set upon, robbed and murdered. All too much of that sort of thing goes on at the present time, and the police seem powerless to prevent it. However, what happened, however unfortunately, to Mr Palgrave during a weekend, has nothing to do with his work here. The whole thing has led to considerable unrest in the staff commonroom and given rise to a most undesirable degree of speculation and excitement among my boys and girls. I really cannot countenance further disruption.'

'All I need is five minutes' conversation with Mr Winblow, sir, and it will be less noticeable if I have it here than if I go to his private address or ask him to come down to the station.'

'Oh, very well.' He rang through to his secretary. 'Chase up Mr Winblow, please, Mrs Wrack, and ask him to spare me a moment. He should be in the history room with 4A. I suppose,' he added to the sergeant, 'there is no objection to my being present at this interview? It will enable me to determine whether Winblow ought to have a solicitor to watch his interests. He is a young, inexperienced man and may need professional advice.'

'Remain by all means, sir. You may be able to help both Mr Winblow and my enquiry.' They waited in silence until Winblow appeared.

'You sent for me, Headmaster?'

'Sit down, Winblow, and remember that you are not obliged to answer any of the sergeant's questions unless you wish.'

'You were aware that Mr Palgrave had written a book – his second book – I believe, sir?' asked the sergeant.

'Yes, of course. A very bright chap, poor Palgrave.'

'We learn that he had various copies made of it.'

'Oh, yes. I've got one, a carbon.'

'Was it a gift to you?'

'Not a gift, no. He said he'd like me to read it, so long as I didn't spill tea on it or get it dogeared. Then I was to keep it somewhere safe until he asked for it in case he needed it to check by, or to send to another publisher.'

'Somewhere safe?'

'Yes. He said the copy he'd sent in could get lost or damaged and the copy he was keeping at his digs – well, there might be a fire or a burglary. He was pretty steamed up about the work. Said it was a major *opus* and would establish him for all time. Very euphoric, and all that.'

'Have you read your copy, sir?'

'Not yet. Thought I'd get on to it in the Easter holiday. Not much time for reading during term,' said Mr Winblow, with one eye on his headmaster.

'Do you know what happened to the other copies, sir?'

'Not a clue. Nobody else on the staff here has one, that's for sure.'

'Thank you, sir. That's all, then.'

The head nodded dismissal to the assistant master and, when the door had closed behind Winblow, he said:

'Are you satisfied, Sergeant?'

'Oh, yes, sir, thank you. It was a very minor point, but we have to clear these things out of the way.'

'There's a letter from a Mrs Kirby,' said the detective-inspector upon his subordinate's return. 'She wants to tell us something which she thinks may have a bearing.'

'Let's hope it's something useful, sir. You were right not to make anything important out of the missing copies. Apparently he distributed them among his friends for safe keeping, as I think you said.'

'Well, you'd better get along and see what this woman has to say. Here's the address. Any time after six, she says.'

'Lives in Chelsea, I notice, sir. Means she may know something.'

'You're thinking of the river. I thought of it, too.'

'Would a body chucked in the river, perhaps over one of the bridges, fetch up as far as the Bregant Docks, sir? It was opposite them that the body was found. There's a big bend in the river after Hammersmith.'

'Our river chaps would know about that, I expect, but, if you ask me, Old Father Thames is quite unpredictable. Besides, the fact that this woman lives near the river may be coincidence, so it's no good raising our hopes too high that she really knows anything important.'

* * *

Miranda welcomed the young sergeant with the kindly warmth she extended to all visitors and offered him a drink.

'Not just now, thank you, madam. I understand you have something to tell us which may have a bearing on the case of murder we are investigating.'

'I don't know whether it's important, but, in case you didn't know about it, I thought perhaps I should tell you.'

The sergeant took out his notebook.

'Fire away, madam,' he said encouragingly, so Miranda, aided at times by Adrian, gave a full account of the holiday at Saltacres and the death of young Camilla Hoveton St John. The sergeant did not interrupt her, but dotted down his shorthand in the hope that something useful might emerge from the long narrative.

'Thank you, madam,' he said when she appeared to have come to an end. 'In your opinion, then, Mr Palgrave's death could have been a revenge job.'

'I can't think of any other reason why anybody should have killed him. You see, the more I thought about it – it doesn't matter telling you this now that he's dead – and the more we talked it over, my husband and I, the more I was convinced that nobody but Colin could have drowned Camilla.'

'That's very interesting, madam. Thank you for your help.' He returned to his headquarters and retailed the interview. 'I can't see there's much in it, sir,' he said. 'We had a report on the Saltacres case, of course, but I can't see any real tie-up. The Saltacres case was never brought in as murder. They are not even certain which day the girl was drowned, and it seems open to doubt whether anybody was with her at the time, anyway.'

'Well, we must still have a shot at finding out where Palgrave went that Friday night. Once we know that, we really can get weaving. Until we know it we are only groping in the dark. If only we could find a motive for his death we might get somewhere, too, but I can't believe, from your report, that this woman has supplied it. The girl died months and months ago.'

'No, I don't think she has helped, sir, but it was worth a try.'

'Did you happen to ask her whether she had been lent one of the copies of the novel?'

'No, sir. Judging by what the schoolmaster chap told me, I didn't think it important. Besides, she only knew Palgrave through this girl picking him up on a holiday beach. I got the impression that she'd (Mrs Kirby, I mean) that she'd seen very little, if anything, of him once the holiday was over. After all, they live a good way apart and wouldn't have very much in common, anyway. As you will see when I've typed out my report, sir, I asked her point blank if Palgrave had visited her that Friday night. She looked astonished and said he had not. Besides, he's got a car, sir, and his landlady's got a garage. It's quite a way from Finchley to Chelsea. He would have driven to her flat, sir, if he'd gone there at all, not walked.'

'So what about trains and buses? It could be confirmed that he left on foot, but suppose he used public transport? If Mrs Kirby was lying, and he *did* go to Chelsea that evening, he may well have preferred a bus rather than take his car across London. Of course we've tried that line, but it might be as well to have another go.'

'A chap of Palgrave's age would have taken his car, sir, and chanced finding somewhere to park at the other end. We know he didn't take a taxi. We've sorted that out. Anyway, the impression I got was that Mrs. Kirby was telling the truth and that she'd seen little or nothing of Palgrave since the holiday.'

'Well, ring her up and find out whether she has a copy of his book. If she has, ask whether he brought it to her himself or sent it by post. Rattle her a bit, if you can. Something might come out. When you've done that, we'll go over my interviews with Palgrave's agents and publishers. I don't see any use I can make of what they told me, but perhaps you can make some suggestions.'

Miranda, it transpired, had received a photo copy of *Lost Parenthesis* by post, together with a request that she would keep it safely and return it if Palgrave asked for it back. She said she had begun to read it when it arrived, thought the early chapters were pretentious and not very interesting and that she had then turned to the last couple of pages and promised herself a full study of the book later on, as Palgrave seemed in no hurry to have her copy back. Asked if she knew where any other copies were likely to have gone, she suggested that one might have been lent to the Lowsons.

'We met them on holiday. Colin was once engaged to Morag,' Miranda said, and gave the sergeant the Lowsons' new address to which they had moved when they left London soon after the Saltacres holiday.

'Right up there?' said Pinhurst, when he heard where they were living. 'Oh, well, that puts them right off the map so far as our enquiry is concerned. I'll tell you what, though. We've got his own carbon copy among his other stuff. I'm going to plough through it again and then you can have a go. You'll understand why when I tell you about my interviews with Peterheads and Kent and Weald.'

The offices of Peterhead and Peterhead were in a turning off the Strand, and Pinhurst had gone to them before he tackled Kent and Weald. The agents were father and son and it was the younger partner who was interviewed.

He produced the top copy which Palgrave had sent them and also the letter which had accompanied the typescript. In it Palgrave stated that the book had taken longer to write than he had anticipated, but that here it was at last. There was also a copy of the letter they had sent back to him, promising to read the book, to which they had been looking forward, and to let him have their opinion of it if, for any reason ('as it is only your second novel') they thought it unsuitable for offer to Kent and Weald.

Then there was another letter:

'Please do not proceed with *Lost Parenthesis* until you hear from me again. Checking the carbon copy, I have come to the conclusion that my description of some of the chief characters may be libellous.'

Pinhurst was intrigued and asked whether, in the agent's opinion, there was any substance in Palgrave's fears. He was assured that in the opinion of the agents there was, on the surface, no substance in them at all, unless the author had had some specific persons in mind and, even so, it was very doubtful indeed whether any of the statements in the book were actionable.

'After we had written to him in answer to his letter when he sent us the book, we got his second letter asking us not to send the work to Kent and Weald. We tried to telephone him, but he was at school during our office hours, so we wrote another letter. I suppose that, by the time it was delivered, he was dead. We don't know what to do about the book now. We are not prepared to ignore what must be regarded as the author's last wishes, so we are holding on to the script in case he left any posthumous papers which can solve our problem. Possibly his next-of-kin may give us permission to go ahead with the book.'

The prospective publishers had even less to say. They had been rung up by Peterheads with the information that the author wanted to withdraw his book and had been surprised and rather regretful. They had lost money ('as we expect to do on a first book, Detective-Inspector') but they thought Mr Palgrave had talent. They had been given the title of his second book and a short synopsis of the plot, both sent in earlier by the author.

'No sense in pursuing any more of these sidelines,' said Pinhurst, 'until we've found out where he went after he left the school on that Friday afternoon. I detest these chase-ups. Just a lot of dead ends to follow and dead wood to get rid of and, ten to one, no dice in the end. Oh, well, let's get back to the landlady and that old nosey parker next door, and then we'll have another go at your Mrs Kirby. I think she is our best bet, because if there is a tie-up between the death of the St John girl and Palgrave being given a lethal dose of arsenic, well, she's the only person, apart from her husband, who seems to have known both parties.'

'There are also the Lowsons, sir.'

'Yes, if they still lived in London, but Mrs Kirby gave you a Lancashire address.'

'People don't always stay put in their homes, sir.'

'Oh, well, if we get nothing in these parts, we must have a go at the Lowsons. Didn't Mrs Kirby tell you that Lowson is a doctor, though? Doctors don't gallivant all over the place when they've got their own practice. Palgrave was poisoned in London, not in Lancashire.'

'*Cherchez la femme,* sir? And, according to Mrs Kirby, Dr Lowson sold his practice after he lost his father, and is engaged in research.'

CHAPTER 17

A DEAD MAN SPEAKS

'My fancies, fly before ye;
Be ye my fiction – but her story.'
Richard Crashaw

Dame Beatrice read her photocopy of *Lost Parenthesis* with more concentrated attention than she usually accorded to works of fiction; in fact, by the time she began the third chapter she was inclined to think that here was part of an autobiography rather than a slightly over-written piece of purely imaginative prose.

This impression was heightened by the fact that the narrative was told in the first person singular and that the writer, somewhat irritatingly, took himself very seriously indeed.

Not risking a disclosure of his true profession, Palgrave had described himself as a young interne and, although parts of the story appeared to have been plagiarised (whether the author realised it or not) from other and better writers, there was no doubt that he had done his homework by consulting non-fictional works on medicine, the law and morbid psychology.

The theme of the book was blackmail. The hero had found himself involved with a woman patient described as a few years older than himself. He had yielded to her charms to the extent of providing her with a baby whom, at her instigation, he had subsequently murdered.

On the strength of this (Dame Beatrice thought) unlikely episode, since to procure an abortion for the woman in these conscienceless days would have been a simpler and far less dangerous proposition that the calculated infanticide of a being already delivered from the womb, the mother blackmailed the young medico, bleeding him so mercilessly that he had seen fit to drown her.

This had happened on holiday and here the author had taken further risks. Under fabricated names, Saltacres and Stack Ferry were well, although over elaborately, described, and the characters, to anybody who knew the originals, were all too plainly not only Palgrave himself, but his acquaintances, including Miranda, Adrian, Morag and the dead Camilla.

The latter, indeed, appeared in several rôles, or so it seemed to the percipient reader. She was both the predatory blackmailer and the hoydenish teenager. She also appeared to be a kind of Siamese twin of the apparently idolised (by the author) heroine, whom the first-person hero ended by marrying.

Incidents which Dame Beatrice knew of only by hearsay, such as the misappropriated car, the moonlight bathes, the bohemian set-up at the Saltacres cottage and the coincidental arrival at the cottage of Morag and Cupar Lowson (here renamed Nancy and Shaun McBride) would mean little, she thought, to readers who had never taken a peep behind the scenes, but might act like dynamite on anybody who had the facts which lay behind the incidents described in the book.

On the other hand, the descriptions of the various characters and the actions and motives attributed to each were so mixed and mingled and, in the reader's view, often so impulsive and contradictory, that it was unlikely that any one person would have been able to identify herself or himself as a personage portrayed in the book.

'No truth, no libel, I imagine,' said Dame Beatrice, handing the script to Laura. 'See what you make of it. Knowing as much as I do, and a good deal more which I surmise, I do not feel that I have brought an open mind to my perusal of this work. You, I trust, will do better.'

'Doubtful,' said Laura. 'By this time I expect you've told me much of what you've found out, and you know what my mind is like — it is apt to fill in gaps. Is the book, as a book, worth reading?'

'There, again, I can hardly tell. It is the book of an inexperienced author, but the story might interest some people and it is well, if somewhat elaborately, written.'

'But you wouldn't put it on your library list?'

'As a contribution to my study of morbid psychology, perhaps I would.'

Laura took a couple of evenings to read the script. When she returned it. she said,

'Could be hot stuff if you equated yourself with one or two of the characters, I suppose. That's if you could get yourself disentangled from the various ladies involved. Naturally I've tried to sort out Camilla St John from Miranda Kirby from Morag Lowson from any of Camilla's girlfriends, but it can't be done, and the same goes for Palgrave himself, Adrian Kirby, Lowson, and the various medicos who, I suppose, are composite portraits of the schoolmasters Palgrave knew. Quite the nastiest bit of work seems to be Palgrave himself, as the book is written in the first person. In any case, the plot is wildly improbable.'

'It can't be, you know,' said Dame Beatrice, 'if somebody thought it so probable that he or she went to the length of poisoning the author. I think I will show the book to Ferdinand.'

'A man – the only one – who really terrifies me. If ever I am had up for serious crime, I pray I don't come up against him.'

'Oh, he is usually defending. He says it is far more fun than prosecuting and a great deal more·difficult, too, because the prisoner usually *has* done it and to convince a jury that he has *not,* is a task of some magnitude.'

Sir Ferdinand read the book and asked what he was supposed to do about it.

'Could it lead to the murder of the author?' his mother enquired.

'Only by the critics. Is this the arsenic victim?'

'Yes, indeed. It is all mixed up with that other case in which I was involved, the death by drowning at Saltacres.'

'As I see it, the main theme of the story is blackmail. The death of the girl seems to have been incidental to the main plot.'

'Yes, but, by inference, the hero drowned her.'

'On the assumption that, as has been so glibly and yet somewhat truly said, each man kills the thing he loves. How much, and to what an unfathomable extent, writers are the products of the age into which they are born! Kipling would have been twice as good had he lived at the present day; Shakespeare less than a quarter as great, had he come on earth a century or so later than he did.' He cocked an eye at Laura, but she refused to be drawn into contention.

'So you see no reason why Palgrave should have been murdered?' said Dame Beatrice.

'Oh, yes, I do. *Somebody* saw something in the story which threatened him.'

'Him?'

'Or her, but as the book is written in the first person by a man and, very obviously, from a man's point of view, I am inclined to think that "him" is the operative word. The book, in fact, may well be Palgrave's confession, and his death, in spite of what the police think, may have been an expiatory suicide.'

'I might agree, if he had not also been responsible for trying to get the book suppressed. That seems to me extraordinary in the face of his letter to me.'

'Somebody who, like you, has read the script, may be his murderer, then.'

'And that would *include* me, as I first saw the book before Palgrave died. He wanted me to give it my blessing, as I think I told you. But I am still at a loss. His letter which accompanied the script hardly seems to me to contain a request that an author who wanted to suppress his book would make.'

'I wonder what his first book was like,' said Laura. 'Any use to get hold of a copy and compare them? Means the public library, I expect. It will be out of print by now, no doubt, and we don't even know who his publishers were, do we?'

'Mr Pinfold will know,' said Dame Beatrice. 'He will have taken possession of all Palgrave's papers. It may be helpful to read his first book, although very few first novels do anything except give some clue to the author's opinion of himself, for most must, of necessity, be autobiographical.'

'Palgrave's second book is that, too, in a manner of speaking, as I think we are agreed,' said Ferdinand. 'I wonder whether a talk with his publishers would be helpful?'

* * *

The publishers were cautious, though courteous when she visited them, and did not attempt to offer any help in suggesting a reason for Palgrave's death.

'Naturally, the murder of one of our authors is not the kind of publicity we look for,' said the senior partner. 'All the same, we are somewhat disappointed that Colin saw fit to withdraw his second book. We should have been interested to see it. When he had ironed out some rather regrettable mannerisms and pruned an extensive and dictionary-conscious vocabulary, he might have shown considerable promise. We were quite prepared to take a chance on his second book unless it was very bad indeed.'

'I thought, when I read his two books, that he had talent,' said Dame Beatrice.

'Oh, you've seen the second one, then?'

'He sent me a copy in the hope that I would write a preface, I think. Do you know why Mr Palgrave decided to withdraw the book from publication? It seems a mystery to me.'

'We have no idea. His agents sent us a copy of his letter, but it is very short and offers no explanation of his action.'

'Did you know him well?'

'He came here several times. He was a very eager and enthusiastic author, of course, and expected rather more from his first book than was justified by the standard of his work, and by the fact that it was his initial attempt and by no means in the best-seller class, but his attitude was no phenomenon in our experience.'

'Were you surprised when you knew that he did not wish to publish his second book?'

'We were more than surprised. He had been in correspondence with us about the book, giving us a synopsis first of all, and in later letters giving us more details of the plot and a great deal of unnecessary information as to the book's progress in its later stages. He seemed altogether delighted with the work. The very last thing we expected was a complete *volte-face*. We are at a loss to understand it.'

'I suppose – I advance the theory with all diffidence – I suppose the letter to his agents postponing, or, as I understand it, forbidding publication, *did* come from Mr Palgrave himself, and not from some outside source?'

'Such an idea has never occurred to us, nor, I am sure, to Peterheads. Who would take such a liberty?'

'Either a practical joker or somebody who had an interest in suppressing the book.'

'You say you have read the book, Dame Beatrice. Could there be such an interest?'

'I hardly know. Blackmail is one of the themes explored in the story, and from previous knowledge which I assimilated from his acquaintances, I know that Mr Palgrave was not averse to including real incidents and real personalities in his narrative. I should be interested to see your copy of the letter which was sent to his agents.'

'I begin to see that there are possibilities we had not considered, but if the law of libel had been infringed, surely it would have paid the objector better, had we published the book, to take us to court rather than to prevent publication altogether?' He smiled benevolently. 'Not that we should have published, of course, if we had had any doubts.'

Less inhibited, less dignified and perhaps less cautious than the senior partner of Kent and Weald, young Mr Peterhead put the cards on the table in no uncertain manner.

'K and W,' he said, 'would have published the book. It's not bad. Palgrave would have shown lots of promise once he could have forgotten that he was a schoolmaster. Apart from that, there would have been the posthumous fame of getting himself murdered. Very sorry about that, of course, but it would have helped sales no end. Still, it cuts both ways. *Lost Parenthesis* might have sold well on the strength of the author's violent death, but, with no more books to come — well, t'other or which, I suppose, in the end. Not that I want to sound callous or materialistic, of course.'

'Did you ever check to find out whether Mr Palgrave's last letter was genuine?'

'Genuine? How do you mean, Dame Beatrice? It had his signature on it all right.'

'Did you not think it strange that he should wish to suppress his novel?'

'Oh, authors are the queerest lot of people in the world. You'd be amazed at what we and their publishers have to put up with. I talked the letter over with my father and we decided to take no action for a week or two in the hope (and full expectation, I may add) that Palgrave would change his mind. By the time (as we'd heard nothing more) we had decided to write to him regretting his decision, hoping he had changed his mind and would instruct us to go ahead and send the book to Kent and Weald, we had the news that he was dead, so nothing further has been done, of course.'

'That is very interesting. May I see his last letter to you? As I told you when I asked for this interview, I am accredited to the Home Office and am accustomed to working in co-operation with the police.'

'Of course you may see his letter. The police have seen it and were surprised not to find an answer to it from us, but all we did was to telephone him. Our call was never answered except by his landlady. He was never at home during our office hours.'

'He was dead, of course, by the time you wrote to him.' She took the letter which young Mr Peterhead had extracted from a filing-cabinet. 'I see that this is not dated. You would not remember what the postmark on the envelope was?'

'I'm afraid not. I remember that the letter came by second-class post, though.'

'Was that unusual?'

'Yes, under the circumstances. That is why I remember it. One would suppose that if he didn't want us to send his book to Kent and Weald he would either have telephoned or told us by first-class post. There would have been very little time to lose if he really wanted us to suppress the book and not let K and W have it.'

'He could have written direct to the publishers himself, I suppose, though, asking them to return the book to him when they had received it from you.'

'It does all seem a bit mysterious, because of course he could have done that.'

'I would like to submit this letter to a handwriting expert, together with any other signatures of Mr Palgrave's which you may have. It might also be interesting to find out whether this letter and the others were typed on the same machine.'

'How about fingerprints?' asked young Mr Peterhead, entering into the spirit of the thing with interest and considerable zest.

'Useless, I fear. None of the fingerprints on this letter will be on record, with the exception of my own.'

'Yours?' The young man looked astonished and disbelieving. Dame Beatrice spread out a yellow claw.

'There are times when mine have to be distinguished from those of the felons whose fraudulent documents I am called upon sometimes to handle,' she explained. 'I would like to repeat a previous question in slightly different words. I think I may receive a more significant answer from you this time. Now, Mr Peterhead, what was your reaction when you first read this letter? Granted, as you say, that authors are kittle cattle, what did you think of Palgrave's request?'

'As you see, it was not so much a request as an order. We were astounded. As a whole, authors are proud of their work and extremely jealous that it shall be appreciated by others to the extent that they appreciate it themselves. The point at which an author begins to think his stuff is no good, and wonders why he ever committed himself to writing it, is about two-thirds of the way through. By the time he's got over that hurdle and finished the book, he's convinced that the world has produced another genius and that his book is a masterpiece.'

'And Palgrave, in that sense, was not noticeably different from the norm?'

'Definitely not, I would say. We couldn't understand his reactions. We concluded he was tired, that's all. We knew he had had trouble, at the beginning, in getting down to the book, and, of course, he was combining authorship with another very demanding job.'

'Schoolmastering is what you make of it,' said Dame Beatrice. 'The better the author, the worse the schoolmaster, perhaps.'

'Then Palgrave wasn't too bad a schoolmaster,' said the literary agent. Dame Beatrice clicked her tongue and Peterhead laughed, but they both came back to the matter in hand when she said:

'Well, perhaps you will mark this letter in some way so that you will know it again when I return it. I will give you a receipt for it, of course. There is one other small matter. The police have found a receipted bill from a typewriting agency for a top copy and two carbon copies of Palgrave's book. There is also a receipted bill for two photo copies. We think we can account for all of these. Only one item seems to be unaccounted for. We have not found Palgrave's own manuscript or typescript from which the other copies must have been made.'

'Wouldn't he have kept it by him?'

'Apparently not. We can trace the other copies. He kept one, two of his friends have theirs and one came to me, but of the original copy there is no sign.'

'In a safe deposit somewhere?'

'I hope not. If it is, my theories may be useless. One other point, and I daresay it is not of the least importance: Palgrave seems to have typed all his letters to you. Is that not so?'

'Yes, indeed it is. Like the one in your hand, all his letters to us were in typescript apart from the signature.'

'But his novel was typed by an agency, yet he himself had a typewriter.'

'Oh, that's not unusual. Some of our authors like to send in a professional-looking copy and others shy away from the labour of making a fresh draft of a whole novel when they have finished the book. There is nothing extraordinary in the fact that Palgrave went to an agency. For one thing, a lot of people hate the fiddling business of dealing with carbons. I suppose it *is* a bit of a nuisance.'

'Thank you, but that does not clear up my small point. I feel he is unlikely to have destroyed his own typescript. It must be somewhere, but we have not found it. Ah, well, now to get this signature examined.'

The tests took a little time, but the result of them justified her theories. Two handwriting experts who often found themselves on opposite sides in trials for forgery were for once in positive agreement. The evidence afforded by a comparison of the agents' letter with the other letters supplied to Dame Beatrice was equally satisfactory. The signature on the withdrawal letter was not by the same hand as the signatures on three letters which had been sent to the publishers, neither had this key letter which forbade publication of the novel been typed on the machine the police had found in Palgrave's lodgings.

'So now,' said Dame Beatrice to Laura, 'to the telephone to get the police to track down the missing copy.'

'As it's the original draft which is missing,' said Laura when Dame Beatrice had telephoned, 'it seems to me it wouldn't hurt to have me go along to that typing bureau – the police will have found the address among Palgrave's things – and find out whether perhaps they know what happened to the original script. They must have had it to make the copies he ordered.'

'Oh, I have told the police that I have no doubt as to who has the original draft. Mrs Lowson has it. There is every reason why she should have been sent that special very personal copy of the novel. I only hope she enjoyed reading it more than we did.'

'Would she have recognised herself?'

'There's the telephone!' said Dame Beatrice.

The call was from Adrian Kirby. The police had just left his flat. They had asked for the Lowsons' Lancashire address. He had had no option but to disclose it. He hoped he had done right. He had been alone in the flat because Miranda was at the art school.

Dame Beatrice, to whom Laura had handed the receiver, reassured him. She knew why the police wanted to get in touch with the Lowsons, she said. They were trying to trace a copy of Palgrave's book. Somebody who must have read it had been attempting to suppress it.

'But that implicates Miranda and me,' said Adrian.

'And Laura Gavin and my son and myself, not to mention a fellow teacher to whom Mr Palgrave had lent a copy, and, of course, anybody who may have been shown a first draft of the novel before it was retyped, or even one of the typists at the agency,' said Dame Beatrice.

'All the same, I shall ring up the Lowsons and warn them to expect a visit from the police.'

'I cannot prevent your doing that, but I advise against it.'

'The Lowsons are our friends and there is little Camilla's death to consider. Miranda and I have talked and talked about that. One of us who was at the cottage that night must have carried Camilla's suitcase to the dunes and tried to hide it there so that it would appear that she had gone off with somebody else and left us. It must have been taken out of the cottage after her death, not before. There would have been no need to remove it while she was still alive. It was the act of a guilty person.'

'Do you think Colin Palgrave was that guilty person?'

'We wondered, but his own death seems to let him out.'

'I think,' said Dame Beatrice, rejoining Laura, 'that I will go and see the Lowsons myself. It will be interesting to find out which of Mr Palgrave's private readers saw fit to suppress the book, and as the narrator of the story is supposed to be a doctor the Lowsons may be promising material.'

'I don't suppose Dr Lowson himself would bother to read the typescript of a third-rate novel,' said Laura, 'but I bet *Mrs* Lowson has read it.'

CHAPTER 18

THE MUDFLATS, AMPLETIDE SANDS

'Three corpses lay out on the shining sands,
In the morning gleam as the tide went down.'
Charles Kingsley

Laura Gavin had never lacked valour; under Dame Beatrice's tutelage she had learned caution and discretion. When a second call came from Adrian Kirby to say that he had conferred with his wife and they had decided to let the Lowsons know that a visit from the police was impending, Laura informed him that Dame Beatrice was out and she did not know when to expect her back, but that she would deliver his message as soon as Dame Beatrice returned. Then she rang up Pinhurst.

'Dame Beatrice has gone to Lancashire,' she said, 'and I don't trust those Lowsons.'

As she was the wife of an Assistant Commissioner and therefore, in police opinion, an honorary member of the Force, Pinhurst listened patiently and promised that Dame Beatrice's safety would be taken care of, and that he would make liaison with the Lancashire lads. Comforted, Laura thanked him and rang off, but in less than an hour he rang her.

'What is Dame Beatrice's object in going to see the Lowsons?' he asked. 'They can't be implicated, living where they do. Do you think she has got on to something?'

'I don't think so, if you're talking about Palgrave's death. She is trying to find out who forged that letter to his agents. She thinks it may be a pointer, that's all. And, of course, she's on the track of the original copy. She thinks the Lowsons may have it, as the book is dedicated to M, and Mrs Lowson's name is Morag and she and Palgrave were once engaged to be married.'

'Well, we've had a go at the Kirbys and at that young schoolmaster who seems to have been given a copy, and the Lowsons are next on our list, but there was nothing actionable in the book. I've read it myself, and a bigger lot of claptrap and balderdash I've never had to wade through. Apart from the forged letter, we've still got plenty on our plate down here. We still don't know where Palgrave got to on that Friday evening. The locals have checked out all the hotels within miles of where his body was found, but there isn't a thing. We've tried all the people at his school and he certainly did not visit any of them. When he was seen leaving his digs by that neighbour, he had nothing with him but a fairly large briefcase.'

'Big enough to hold pyjamas and his shaving tackle, if he was going to spend the night somewhere. It's all my husband brings when he comes to spend a night with me at the Stone House, and quite often he does not bother about the pyjamas,' said Laura. 'He can always get into a pair of mine if it's cold – the trousers, anyway – and I can always lend him a sweater.'

'Oh, Lord! If he spent the night – or was prepared to – it could have been anywhere, except that he didn't take his car. I wonder whether somebody picked him up? We've tried London Transport and the taxi-drivers.'

Upon arrival at her hotel, which was on a slope above the shores of Ampletide Sands, a small resort on the long inlet which runs past Cartmel out of Morecambe Bay, Dame Beatrice had rung up the Lowsons to ask when (not whether) she might call. She had been invited to come on the following afternoon.

After lunch on that day she went down the long drive of the hotel, through pleasant woods, (the hotel stood in its own grounds), to the sea-front. As she strolled along a concreted promenade made extremely narrow because a railway line ran directly behind it, she surveyed the expanse of shining mud left by the tide and then, stopping to apostrophise an oyster catcher and aware of the warning notices which had been put up all along the sea-wall, she said to the handsome, red-legged bird:

'Well, wader, scavenging for molluscs, crustaceans and worms, I think the waters here must resemble those of the Solway. Perhaps you remember Sir Walter Scott's ballad of *Young Lochinvar?* "Love swells like the Solway and ebbs like its tide". How true, in so very many cases! I wonder whether it applies in this one? Could it have been malice aforethought which caused poor Colin Palgrave to dedicate his book to his lost love, or was it intended only as a reminder of what may have been "an old passion" and meant only as a tribute to that? More likely, I think. The book is pretentious, but not malicious.'

The bird, suddenly aware of her presence, although not of being addressed, uttered a shrill, protesting *klee-eep, klee-eep,* ran rapidly across the mud and then, tucking away its long red legs, it took off with low flight and shallow wingbeats, changed its note to a slightly trilling and a shorter call and put distance between itself and the intruder.

Dame Beatrice, with a suspicious look at the distant sea, then focused her attention upon a dark mass on the edge of the deceptively mild-mannered water. She said to the sea: 'My name is King Canute. Stay where you are!'

The sands (so called in the brochures) were firmer than she had expected. At a surprising pace for so extremely elderly a lady, she crossed them and then knelt at the sodden sea-verge to examine the body. A very brief inspection was enough. It was a dead body and one which she recognised. She made all speed back to the hotel and telephoned the police. They rang back within the hour.

'Papers of identification on the body confirm your theory, Dame Beatrice, ma'am. There was a suicide note. Took prussic acid, it says, only it calls it hydrocyanic acid. Quick, that's one thing. Good on you, ma'am, for recognising the body, if you'd only seen him once before, and some time ago and alive, at that. We'll need you for the inquest, ma'am, I'm afraid.'

'Come in,' said Morag. 'You said something about a book.'

'Colin Palgrave's novel. I believe you have a copy of it,' said Dame Beatrice.

'Oh, that!'

'I also have a copy. From the dedication to M, I deduced that the book was written especially for you.'

'Good gracious, no! Through here, Dame Beatrice, and then we can look out on to the garden. I don't suppose the dedication was meant for me at all, although, of course, at one time— '

'Yes, so I have been told. He wanted me to write a preface to the book. You can help me. The work appears to be autobiographical. Would that be so?'

'Goodness knows!'

'And I thought perhaps you could tell me whether it throws any light upon the manner of his death.'

'But we know the manner of his death. Miranda Kirby sent me a cutting from the local paper. He died of arsenical poisoning, didn't he? I think poor Colin committed suicide. Arsenic is easy enough to come by. There are weed-killers, flypapers, all sorts of things.'

'So that is why arsenic was chosen, because it is easy to come by. It is also easily administered. The powdered form can be disguised in a cup of black coffee, especially to a man already under the influence of narcotics, perhaps, or drink.'

Morag had been standing at the window overlooking the garden. She turned round and went across the room to a bookcase from which she took a brown paper parcel.

'Here is my copy of the book, if that is what you came for,' she said. 'Are they going to publish it after all?'

'Not unless you are willing to admit to a forged letter.'

Morag put the parcel down on to a small table, went unsteadily to an armchair and sat down.

'So you know,' she said. 'How *much* do you know?'

'Everything, I think, but I like to check my findings. The signature on the letter is known to have been forged. Mr Palgrave was murdered before he could repudiate the letter and ask that publication should go ahead as planned. Where did you stay on the night of his death? You may, I think, have been somewhere in London. The police are still trying to trace his movements on that night.'

'They can go on trying. Why should I tell you anything?'

'There is no reason why you should. If you choose to keep your own counsel, the law must take its course, that is all.'

'You mean I'll be charged with forgery? Oh, but it was such a little thing I did! It isn't like forging a cheque or a will, is it?'

'I think perhaps it is worse. No doubt Mr Palgrave was proud of his book and was looking forward to seeing it in print and perhaps reading favourable notices about it in the press.'

'It's a dangerous book; a harmful book. I *had* to do what I did. I don't know how Colin found out, but apparently he did. I suppose that girl told him things.'

'I think, you know,' said Dame Beatrice, taking the armchair opposite Morag, 'that you had better do as I say, and tell me the whole story.'

'In my own words, leaving out no detail, however slight?' said Morag, with an attempt at a lightheartedness which obviously she did not feel. 'Oh, well, if you know I forged the letter, I suppose I can expect trouble.'

'Not for forging the letter. That can be hushed up, no doubt. Murder, however, cannot be hushed up, and I have come here to talk about *two* murders. You have admitted to forgery—'

'What I admit to you in this room is not evidence. I understand why Catholics go to Confession, though, so I will clear my conscience. I'm sorry about Colin, but he shouldn't have written that book. It *had* to be suppressed. He knew far too much. The book opened my eyes to all sorts of things I had half wondered about, but had never dared to face. Anyway, I am *not* sorry about that little blackmailer. I had no idea that blackmail was her game until I read Colin's book, but, once I'd read it, all sorts of things dropped into place.'

'I think you give too much credit to Mr Palgrave's knowledge. You mean knowledge about your own affairs and those of your husband, don't you? Mr Palgrave thought of blackmail only because the girl had made a threat to blackmail *him*. I am certain that the story he wrote was based on his knowedge of the girl's character and not on anything he knew of your affairs.'

'But the girl and I are both in the book. I asked Cupar what he thought and he agreed with me and we arranged that I should practise Colin's signature – I had kept his letters to me; they were not, strictly speaking, love-letters, but were all about his first book and the publishers' contract and what he hoped his agents, the Peterheads, might be able to do for him, so there was nothing much in them that I didn't want Cupar to see— '

'Your husband had read the book, then?'

'Well, I could hardly keep it from him. He was appalled by it. He said it could ruin his career if it were published because there were plenty of people able and willing to put two and two together and make five instead of four.'

'I hope I have not done the same thing.'

'Oh, no. You wouldn't be here if you had. I suppose the fact that I was out walking that night, and that the fact the girl was drowned, pointed to me as her murderer.'

'Not necessarily. The facts, so far as they were known, pointed even more clearly to Colin Palgrave. Will you tell me about yourself and him? — and why you think you were the chief suspect for causing Miss St John's death?'

'Why not? I said I wanted to confess. It all began a long time ago. Well, it seems a long time ago now. Colin and I were engaged. He broke it off. He *said* it was because he wanted to give up teaching and become a writer. He *said* that he wouldn't be able to keep a wife and possible children for years and years, and that nobody ought to marry a writer, anyway. They were impossible to live with, he said. He said a lot more along the same lines, but I thought he was tired of me and did not want to say so, and made all these excuses to be rid of me.'

'You may have been right, of course.'

'It did something to me. I had been very fond of him. I could have managed to support both of us until he got established as a writer. I am a trained nurse and I knew I could get a well-paid private job, either with a wealthy invalid or as a doctor's receptionist and dispenser, but I was too proud and too badly hurt to plead or argue. Eventually I met Cupar and we were married.

'Cupar was honest with me up to a point. He told me that a patient of his had had a baby by him. I didn't much mind. I'd had affairs myself before I became engaged to Colin, but I had no idea that Cupar was being blackmailed by the girl. I thought the money he paid out went to support the baby. It wasn't until I read Colin's book that the truth dawned on me, although I suppose I had always had a secret fear that, if the girl ever decided to turn nasty, Cupar's career would be finished. When I had read the book and Cupar had seen it, he had another confession to make. He said his baby had been born, the girl had killed it, and he had written a false death certificate to cover up for her.'

'That, at any rate, was not in Mr Palgrave's book.'

'No, but I was terribly frightened. If people read the book and anybody who had known the wretched girl began to probe, there was no knowing *what* might come out. We agreed that the book must never be published.'

'Well, the forged letter to the agents could hardly have solved that problem for very long. In other words, the author had to die. I am more interested, at the moment, in the death of Camilla St John. Will you tell me exactly what happened that evening?' said Dame Beatrice.

'It didn't really begin with the evening. It began when Cupar and I arrived at the cottage to discover that it had been double-booked for the rest of that week.'

'Such a coincidence that you should have fixed upon the very cottage of which Miss St John was already an inmate.'

'Oh, well, coincidences do occur and the girl was our bad angel, anyway, so I suppose some supernatural force of gravity was at work and pulled us towards her.'

'By the way, had you ever met her before?'

'No, never. Cupar told me who she was as soon as we were alone in the cottage.'

'Please continue.'

'Is there really any need?'

'You said there was virtue in confessing. That is not the reason for my encouraging you to tell me your story. A little later on you will understand why I must hear it. Please trust me. You are not likely to regret it.'

'Adrian and Miranda Kirby think very highly of you. Very well, then. I forged the letter. Do you want to know how I killed the girl?'

'And Colin Palgrave, of course.'

'Colin? Oh, but— '

'Yes, I know you said it was suicide. The police have proof that it was murder.'

'Proof?' Morag at last looked desperately alarmed. 'But they can't have *proof!*'

'I have talked to them on the telephone. I was in contact with them just before I came here.'

'I see.' She got up and walked unsteadily towards the window again. Dame Beatrice's sharp black eyes followed her. She remained staring out into the garden, but the watcher said nothing. 'Oh, well,' said Morag, turning round and resting one tense hand on the wooden ledge, 'here goes, then, if I must. Better the blame should rest on the right shoulders, I suppose.'

'Of course it is. You would not want a smear to remain on Colin Palgrave's memory.'

'But there isn't one, in your opinion, is there?' As though it was difficult to do so, Morag removed her fingers from their grip on the window-ledge and returned to her chair. She leaned back and closed her eyes. Dame Beatrice noted the anxious shadows under them, but felt no compunction in forcing her to talk.

'Go on,' she said. Morag opened her eyes and brushed a hand across them.

'Yes,' she said. 'I'll feel better when I've told you all about it. Well, as soon as Cupar had told me that Camilla was the girl who had had his baby, I saw how impossible the situation was. There was that, and there were Colin and I. It was all such a mix-up that when Colin took us down to the pub that night I thought that a few drinks would help me to decide what to do.'

'But you did not know, at that point, that Miss St John had been blackmailing your husband. You did not know that until you read Mr Palgrave's book and tackled your husband about it.'

'Oh, well, perhaps I had guessed. The drinks didn't really help, so when we went back to the cottage I wrote a note to Camilla telling her to get out or it would be the worse for her. I took it up to her room and pinned it to the pillow. Then I saw her suitcase, so I packed it with everything of hers I could find, waited until Adrian and Miranda were in their room, and then took the suitcase down to the sand-dunes and buried it.'

'Why did you do that?'

'I don't know. Just to be thoroughly bitchy to her, I suppose, and to add a little bit to the warning I'd given her in my note.'

'Ah, yes. Perhaps you had had enough to drink, after all. Where was your husband while all this was going on?'

'In bed and asleep. He had been putting away double whiskies. Whisky always makes him sleepy.'

'Double whiskies? Poor Mr Palgrave!'

'Oh, Colin didn't pay for them after the first round, and Cupar wouldn't have gone on drinking like that if he hadn't been so worried about Camilla's being at the cottage.'

'But she did not accompany the party to the public house?'

'No. She wasn't with us that evening. I was coming back from planting the suitcase when I saw her go up to Colin's car. Then they went off over the marshes and I followed them. I didn't suppose they would hear me, and I took a chance that they wouldn't turn round and see me. I didn't really care, though, whether they did or not. I had as much right on the marshes by moonlight as they had.'

'Surely. Up to that point, then, you did not have murder in mind?'

'No, not until Colin had come out of the water and left her there alone. Then something came over me. I undressed behind a breakwater and swam out to her. She was floating on her back, being rocked very gently by the waves.'

'The tide was still coming in, then?'

'I suppose so. I didn't notice. Then after I had pushed her under and kept her there, I dressed and went back to the cottage.'

'And found your husband still asleep?'

'Yes. Yes, that's right. Cupar was still asleep.'

'Do you remember noticing whether Mr Palgrave's car was still there?'

'I can't remember anything except that the front door was unlatched, so I didn't have to use my key.'

'And when morning came, and both Miss St John and her suitcase had disappeared— ?'

'Oh, the others took it for granted that she had picked up a man and gone off with him.'

'Ah, yes! It was bad luck that the tide brought the body back almost to the spot where it had drowned. Did you never think that Mr Palgrave might be suspected of having made away with the girl?'

'If there had been any trouble for him, I suppose I would have confessed.'

'Now tell me about his death. Where did you stay in London on the night he was given the arsenic?'

'It wasn't in London.'

'Was your husband with you?'

'No. I had read Colin's book— '

'And done what you could to suppress it.'

'Yes. Cupar had to go to a conference — '

'Another one?'

'Oh, well, yes. Since that terrible girl died, Cupar has been engaged in some most valuable research work, so I telephoned Colin and said I wanted to talk to him about the book and asked him to come to Richmond, where I was staying the night, and he came and I slipped the arsenic into his black coffee and that was that.'

'How did his body get on to the Thames mudflats?'

'I tipped it in off the parapet of the bridge.'

'Oh, yes, of course. Your husband knew nothing of this?'

'How could he? He was at his conference, as I told you.'

'And the hotel where you stayed?'

'What does it matter where I stayed?'

Before Dame Beatrice could say more, the door-bell rang. Morag excused herself, adding that it was the servant's free afternoon. She came back with a uniformed sergeant of the county police and, to Dame Beatrice's mild surprise, with Pinhurst.

'I think, Mrs Lowson, you had better sit down,' he said. 'I'm afraid the sergeant has some very bad news for you.'

'But how did you know that her confession was all lies?' asked Laura. 'And what made you ask for the story, anyway?'

'All I wanted was for her to admit that the letter to the literary agents was a forgery. As for her confession to two murders, as soon as the police told her that it was her husband's body which I had found on Ampletide Sands, she retracted it.'

'But why did she make it in the first place?'

'Mistaken idealism plus panic. She was afraid that I had found out the truth, and so I had, of course. She thought that her husband's medical research was far too important for him to be given a life sentence for murder, so she decided to take the rap, as you would say.'

'Good gracious! But *how* did you find out the truth?'

'I began by believing Colin Palgrave's story that he had left Miss St John alive and still enjoying her moonlight bathe and that he had left the cottage that night with his own suitcase and not hers. I was sure that Dr Lowson was *not* in the cottage when Palgrave came in, but returned while the young man was shaving in the kitchen. Then I decided to investigate the only real mystery in the whole affair. There *is* such a thing as coincidence, of course, but, even allowing for all its extraordinary laws, it seemed to me quite outrageous that of all the places there are in which to spend a quiet holiday, the Lowsons should not only have selected the same little village as the Kirbys, whom at that time they had never met, but had even booked the same cottage as that in which Camilla Hoveton St John was staying.'

'So you went to the house agent?'

'And was assured that there had been no mistake over the booking. The holiday cottages are booked only from Saturdays, never mid-week. The Lowsons' tenancy was to begin when the Kirbys' tenancy ended. There was one other small point. I was sure that Lowson was not in bed when Palgrave came in that night, otherwise he would have been aware of a man groping for a suitcase and would have made some remark. Well, then, of course the story of blackmail unfolded itself and the death of Colin Palgrave clinched matters, although I had to find out whether Lowson had read his book. That book could not damage Mrs Lowson directly, but it might – or so Dr Lowson thought – seriously injure his own medical career. Mrs Lowson was persuaded by her husband to invite Palgrave to discuss his book with her. The invitation must have come from her – in fact, when she broke down after hearing that her husband was not only dead, but had left a full confession, she admitted that she had invited Palgrave to spend the weekend with them in their Lancashire home. Dr Lowson was to pick him up in a car near his lodgings and then drive up to Lancashire through the night and return Palgrave to his lodgings on the Sunday evening.'

'So no hotel entered into the arrangements at all!'

'As the police found out. In any case, Lowson would never have risked being seen at a hotel in the company of a man he intended to murder. They would have had coffee and sandwiches in the car as soon as they got out of London. The autopsy showed that arsenic was in both the food and the drink. As soon as Palgrave was taken ill, Lowson drove towards the river – there are alleys wide enough for a car – and dragged the body out of the car and then pushed it over the bank into the Thames.'

'I wonder who cleaned the car? It must have been in a pretty awful mess,' said Laura, practical as ever. 'So Lowson went to Saltacres with the full intention of killing Camilla the blackmailer. How would he know where she was?'

'They would have kept in close touch because of the blackmail payments.'

'So Lowson was a double murderer and committed suicide when the Kirbys warned him that you and the police were on the track. Do you think Palgrave's novel would have given the truth away if ever it had been published?'

'Only to a man with a guilty conscience, and *he* knew the truth already.'

WITHDRAWN
FOR SALE